15.95

22363

# NOTHIN' BUT NET

**DATE DUE**

F
MAN

Mantell, Paul
Nothin' but net

22363

15.95

| DATE DUE | BORROWER'S NAME | |
|----------|-----------------|---|
| | Colleen | |
| | | |
| | | |
| | | |
| | | |

F
MAN

Mantell, Paul
Nothin' but net

MEDIALOG INC
Butler, KY 41006

Selection
Junior Library Guild

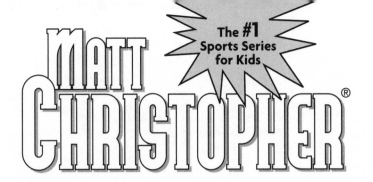

The #1
Sports Series
for Kids

# NOTHIN' BUT NET

**Text by Paul Mantell**

LITTLE, BROWN AND COMPANY

New York ∾ An AOL Time Warner Company

Copyright © 2003 by Catherine M. Christopher

First Edition

The characters and events portrayed in this book are fictitious. Any similarity to real persons, living or dead, is coincidental and not intended by the author.

Matt Christopher® is a registered trademark of Catherine M. Christopher.

Text by Paul Mantell

Library of Congress Cataloging-in-Publication Data

Mantell, Paul.
    Nothin' but net : the #1 sports series for kids / Matt Christopher ; text by Paul Mantell. — 1st ed.
      p.  cm.
    Summary: When thirteen-year-old Tim Daniels gets a chance to go to basketball camp, he is faced with trying to be accepted by the popular players and remaining true to his friend who has become the butt of practical jokes.
    ISBN 0-316-13585-2 (hc) / 0-316-13344-2 (pb)
    [1. Friendship — Fiction.   2. Camps — Fiction.   3. Basketball — Fiction.]   I. Christopher, Matt.   II. Title.

PZ7.M31835No 2003
[Fic] — dc21

2002043339

HC: 10 9 8 7 6 5 4 3 2 1
PB: 10 9 8 7 6 5 4 3 2 1

Q-FF (hc)
COM-MO (pb)

Printed in the United States of America

**T**im Daniels lifted the basketball high over his head. The kid who was guarding him kept reaching out, swatting at it, trying to knock it out of his hands. But Tim was too quick for him. He pivoted first one way, then the other, looking for someone to pass to. No one was free. In that split second, Tim made up his mind to go for the hoop. He faked a pass. The defender took the bait, flailing at the imaginary pass while Tim spun around the other way and drove to the basket.

If he'd been about a foot taller, he might have gone for the slam dunk. But at five feet five inches, there was no way. Tim settled for the layup. "Yes! Five — zip!" he yelled, pumping his fist in the air as he back-pedaled down the court on defense.

At least he wasn't the shortest player on the court. Deivi Alvarez was only five two. But that didn't make

1

Tim feel any better. Deivi was what, twelve? Tim was almost fourteen, and who knew if he had any more inches left in his growth spurt. Yeah, sure, it was cool to be called little sparkplug on the basketball court, but he wished he could lose the little part. It was getting old really fast.

Actually, if it weren't for the fact that he was a good athlete — especially at basketball — most kids would probably have called him a nerd. Slim and compact, with wavy red hair and freckles, Tim was always told he was cute by girls. But the few times he'd actually asked them out, they were never available. He couldn't help feeling they were secretly laughing at him. It made Tim feel even smaller than usual.

He felt best about himself when he did well in school and, of course, when he was on the basketball court. No confusion then. There wasn't another kid his age in the whole neighborhood who could dribble, pass, and drive the lane like he could. Plus he was good on defense — he always had a few take-aways, and even a rebound or two.

So what if he couldn't shoot to save his life? He knew how to sink a layup — and since no one could stop him when he drove to the hoop, what more did he need?

Sure, he'd ridden the bench on the Cougars the past two years. But that was because six-foot-tall Hakim Butler was the school's starting point guard. Butler was graduating in two weeks, though — and come September, Tim had high hopes of moving into Hakim's spot. After all, hadn't he grown five inches just this past year? He understood Coach keeping him on the bench when he'd been five feet tall. But now? Hey, he wasn't that short anymore!

The kid he was guarding got a little careless with his dribble, and Tim was on it like a cat. Tipping the ball away, he raced after it, grabbed it, and tossed it down-court to Kevin Oster, who dunked it with a roar of triumph. Kevin Oster had to be six two, minimum. Dang, thought Tim. What are all these kids eating?

The game ended up 11–2. Of course, it was just an after-school pickup game in the school yard. It counted for nothing, even if it was fun. What really mattered, when it came to basketball, was making the Cougars starting lineup in the fall.

Tim heard a car horn beeping and looked up to see his dad in the minivan, waving. "Coming!" Tim shouted, waving back. He said good-bye to his friends, grabbed his book bag and cap, and ran to the van.

"Hi, Pops," he said, buckling up. "Home from work already?"

"Your mom's got a meeting with her boss, so I took off early."

"Uh-huh."

"So how'd it go?"

"How'd what go? Oh, the game? We won 11–2."

"Wow. Brutal. You ought to take it easy on those poor guys. . . ."

"Dad," Tim said, fighting the urge to smile, "it was just a pickup game. No biggie."

"So listen," his dad said, giving Tim a quick look before he flicked his eyes back to the road. "I've got an idea for you this summer. Wanna hear it?"

"I'm working this summer," Tim reminded him. "At Lotsa Pasta, as a busboy. Remember?"

"Why don't you hear what I'm talking about first," his dad suggested.

"Fine. What?" Tim said, sighing. "I am not going to college-prep camp, Dad. I'm only in seventh grade, okay?"

"I'm not even gonna tell you what it is, if you're going to be so closed-minded."

"All right, all right. What is it?"

"Never mind."

"Come on. Tell me!" Tim demanded, really curious now.

His dad had a distinct twinkle in his eye. "How'd you like to go to basketball camp for the summer?"

"Wh-what do you mean, basketball camp?"

"You learn skills, you compete, I understand the NBA sends some players and coaches to do clinics with the kids . . . oh, never mind. You wouldn't be interested . . ."

"Yes I would!" Tim said. "Are you kidding? The pros come there to teach?" He could see it now — he'd go to this camp whatever-it-was and come back ready for the NCAA, if not the NBA! The Cougars would make him starting point guard for sure.

"You could actually still chill for part of the summer," his dad said. "Mom and I can't afford to send you for the full eight weeks, just for four."

"Fine! Whatever. Just sign me up," Tim said. He was already imagining himself hitting ten foul shots in a row, ten 3-pointers in a row, sinking shots from half-court . . . nothin' but net . . .

"You sure now? I mean, you've never been to sleep-away camp before."

"So what? I'll be playing basketball all day, right?"

"Well, now, I don't know about all day . . ."

"You said it was a basketball camp!"

"Yes, but they have other stuff, too — swimming, softball, arts and crafts, you know, that kind of stuff."

"Oh." Tim considered it for a moment. "Yeah, well, I guess that's okay."

"You still want to go?"

"Uh-huh."

"You sure?"

"I'm sure."

"Because it's very late in the day, and they only have a couple slots left. I've got to sign you up by tomorrow."

Tim shrugged. "So sign me up," he said. "No problem."

"You sure? Last chance to change your mind."

"Dad," Tim said, sighing again but smiling, too, "just do it, okay? I'm not gonna change my mind."

The next day after school, Tim was in the community pool, racing his best friend, Billy Futterman. Billy was five inches taller than Tim and much, much heftier. He wasn't exactly an athlete — in fact, Billy was one of

Tim's "nerd" friends — but he sure could swim. Tim guessed it was Billy's doughy consistency that helped him float. For Tim, swimming was pure struggle. He had practically no body fat, and it was exhausting work just to keep from sinking like a stone.

At the moment, Billy was way ahead of him, and they still had two laps to go. "I quit!" Tim shouted, swimming for the ladder and getting out of the pool.

"Hey," Billy shouted back, suddenly realizing his opponent had quit the race. "What's the matter? Can't take losing?"

"Come on," Tim protested, "you beat me every time, and I still race with you. I'm just tired, is all. I played basketball for three hours yesterday."

Billy swam up and got out of the pool, and the two of them headed for the locker room. "What do you love so much about basketball, anyway? You're not tall enough."

"Shut up, okay? I just like it, that's all."

"Sorry. It's just — well, I mean, you're fast. You could run track or something."

"I grew five inches this past year," Tim pointed out as they dried off and got dressed. "And I'm still hungry every fifteen minutes, so I'm probably still growing."

"And you can't shoot, either. You gonna grow out of that?"

"It just so happens I'm going to basketball camp this summer," he told Billy.

"Oh yeah?"

"Camp Wickasaukee. My dad says it's famous. NBA guys come there and coach you and stuff."

"Well, I'm glad one of us is going to have fun. Me, I'm going to have the summer from hell."

"Huh?"

"My mom and dad decided they're not taking me to Europe with them."

"They're not? I thought you said —"

"They decided I'd be bored, can you believe it? All those dusty old museums and cathedrals. I begged them to take me. Know what my dad said?"

"What?"

"No self-respecting teenager wants to spend the summer traveling with his parents."

"Well," Tim said, shrugging, "you've gotta admit, most kids would rather be doing stuff with kids their age."

"Not me," Billy said. "They're making me go to some camp! Can you believe it?"

"What camp?"

"They don't know yet. Who cares? Camp? Yuck! A whole summer bunking with a bunch of strange kids and a million mosquitoes. Yippee. I'd rather stay home and play video games the whole time." Then he fell silent, lost in thought.

"What?" Tim prodded him.

"I was just thinking . . ." — Billy's face brightened — "maybe I could go where you're going!"

"Huh?"

"Wicka-whatsits."

"Saukee."

"Yeah. Wickasaukee. I mean, I like basketball . . . pretty much. I can't play for beans, but at least I'm tall. I can rebound and block shots and stuff."

"You never even play basketball."

"I do in gym class. You just never see me because you have Gym A and I have Gym B."

"Okay, but I mean, this camp is all about basketball."

"Don't they have other stuff there? Arts and crafts? Swimming?"

"Uh, yeah." Tim was stumped. He couldn't think of any good reason Billy shouldn't come with him to

9

Wickasaukee. Still, he wasn't sure he liked the idea. Billy Futterman and basketball camp were an odd combination. Kind of like fish and ice cream, or peanut butter and nails. In fact, just the thought of it gave Tim a queasy feeling.

That night, Tim, his mom and dad, and his sister, Tara — who was ten years old and unbelievably obnoxious — were sitting in the kitchen having dessert when the phone rang. His mom went and picked up the receiver. "Hello?" She turned to the rest of them and whispered, "It's Elaine Futterman!" Then she listened a lot, nodded a lot, and said, "Uh-huh," "Why not?," and "Great!" a lot, all in her perky, happy voice.

After she hung up, she returned to the table. "Well, guess what?"

Tim took a wild guess. "Billy's coming with me to Wickasaukee?"

"How did you know?" She looked totally amazed. Then she got it. "You two boys talked about it already?"

"Kind of."

"Well, isn't this just fantastic?" his mom said.

Tara silently mimicked her mother with an open

mouth full of food. Tim gave his sister a threatening look, and she cut it out.

"Sounds just about ideal," his dad agreed, smiling broadly. "First time at camp for both of you, isn't it?"

"It sure is," his mom confirmed.

"Yep," said his dad. "Just about ideal."

Tim munched on his apple crumb cake and wondered how ideal it was really going to be — making his grand entrance at basketball camp with Billy Futterman, non–basketball player, attached to his hip. It had the potential to fall way short of ideal.

He forced himself to look on the bright side. At least he wouldn't feel homesick. He'd have a close friend at camp right off the bat.

Yeah, he was probably worried about nothing. Camp Wickasaukee was going to be a blast, with or without Billy Futterman . . . he hoped.

**2**

The day they drove up to Camp Wickasaukee, they stopped first to pick up Billy, whose mom and dad were leaving for Europe that afternoon. Billy's mom kept fussing over him, asking him if he'd remembered to bring his asthma inhaler, and his allergy medicine, and the special insoles for his shoes because he was flat-footed. Tim felt sorry for his friend, listening to her go on like that. Not because of Billy's asthma or allergies or anything like that, but because his mom just wouldn't quit.

"Did you pack the pepperoni sausage I got for you? What about your shower slippers? You don't want to get athlete's foot."

"Would you leave him alone, Elaine?" Mr. Futterman pleaded to no avail. Mrs. Futterman kept it up until Tim's dad beeped the car horn. That seemed to snap her out of it long enough for Billy to make his escape.

"I'm surprised they didn't take you to Europe with them if your mom's so worried about you," Tim said as Billy slid into the backseat, semisquashing him.

"My dad thinks she needs a vacation from me," Billy said.

"Your dad's right," Tim's dad said flatly. "It'll do you both good."

"Now, Peter!" Tim's mom said in a hushed voice. "Keep your opinions to yourself."

"Sorry."

The three-hour ride was peaceful and even pleasant. Billy and Tim spent most of the time playing with Billy's handheld video game system. They found the camp without getting lost, and Billy and Tim started unloading their gear while the grown-ups went inside to sign the paperwork.

While Billy sat on the steps playing his video game, Tim took his first look around at Camp Wickasaukee. It was laid out on a hillside above a long, blue lake. Near the office was the beach, with the swimming areas roped off. Unbroken woods climbed the slopes on the far side of the lake. To the left were softball, soccer, and football fields.

Up the hill and to the right of the office, where the slope flattened out, were dozens of cabins. The larger ones were for the staff. The smaller, more basic ones were for the campers. Nobody had to tell Tim any of this. It was obvious, even to a kid who'd never been to sleep-away camp. As Tim well knew, kids were always on the bottom of the totem pole.

Off to the right, beyond the cabins, were several large, hangarlike buildings. Tim figured this was where they ate and did indoor activities. Up the hill from the ball fields was a huge gym with a Plexiglas roof. Tim could hear dozens of basketballs being dribbled.

A middle-aged, bald-headed man in a blue CAMP WICKASAUKEE T-shirt came over to them. "Hi," he said. "I'm Coach Gabe, the head counselor. And who might you be?"

Tim and Billy introduced themselves and shook hands. "Great, great!" Coach Gabe said. Turning to Billy, he added, "Um, you're going to have to send that home with Mom and Dad. We don't play video games up here — too much good stuff to do!"

Billy looked like he'd just been hit with a sledge-hammer. "What do you mean?" he asked, as if Coach Gabe had been speaking Chinese. "It's mine!"

"And it'll be yours again when you get back home," Coach Gabe assured him. "Don't worry — you'll never miss it."

Billy shot Tim a dubious look. "I can't believe this," he said, his shoulders slumping. "No video? Sheesh."

But Coach Gabe had moved on, to greet Tim's parents as they came down the steps. With a deep sigh, Billy placed the video system gently in Tim's mother's hands. He looked like he was about to cry as the car drove off with his electronic security blanket. Now what am I gonna do? he wondered.

"Come on," Tim said, hoisting his duffel bag, "let's go find our bunk."

The building that housed the thirteen-year-old camp-ers was larger than most of the other cabins. In front of the building hung a sign that said EAGLES NEST — Eagles being the name of their age group here. The fourteen-to-fifteen-year-olds lived in Condors Roost, an even larger house higher up the hill. Other cabins — the ones for the younger campers — were farther down the slope and had signs that said CUBS, COLTS, and SPARROWS. Tim wondered what names the girls' bunks had. Probably KITTENS, FAWNS, and BUTTER-FLIES. Sheesh.

Sitting on the steps in front of Eagles Nest was a muscular guy with a blond buzz cut and an orange T-shirt that said HOFSTRA on it. "Hi," he said. "I'm Jody, your counselor. You guys first-timers, huh?"

"How'd you know?" Billy asked.

"I've been here every summer since I was five," Jody answered, flashing them a brilliant smile. "You're gonna love it. It's the best."

"Yo, Jody!"

They all turned to see a group of four boys approaching, duffel bags slung over their shoulders.

"Hey, you mugs!" Jody called back, flashing that grin again. "How've you been?" They all hugged and high-fived and started talking about people and events Tim knew nothing about. He could see that this was going to go on for a while, so he turned to Billy and said, "Come on, let's go inside."

Eagles Nest was two stories high and had small rooms with two or three beds each. "It doesn't say

16

whose room is whose," Billy said, dropping his duffel bag on the wood floor. "Man, that is heavy. My mom must have put a bunch of bricks in there!"

Another counselor approached them. He had curly dark hair and heavy stubble, as if he hadn't shaved in two days. "Hey, you guys," he said, shaking hands with them. "I'm Tito. Welcome to Eagles Nest."

"Thanks. My name's Tim. Tim Daniels."

"I'm Billy Futterman," Billy said. "Say, where are we supposed to bunk?"

"Let's see," Tito said, whipping a chart out of the back pocket of his shorts. "Billy Futterman? You're in room three." He continued looking at the chart. "Tim Daniels . . . Daniels . . . yep, here you are. Room sixteen."

"Huh?" Billy said, looking suddenly alarmed. "You mean, we're not in the same room?"

"Apparently not. Is that a problem?"

"No!" Tim said quickly, not wanting Tito to think he was a baby or something.

"Yes!" Billy said at the same exact instant. "We were supposed to be together. My mom requested it."

"She did?" Tim said, his eyes wide.

17

"I can switch it around if you want," Tito said.

"Never mind, it's no big deal," Tim assured him. "What the heck, Billy — no biggie, right?"

"I don't know," Billy said, shaking his head and looking at the ground. "My mom was very specific."

Tim frowned. So Billy's mom had made a big deal out of it. He could believe it. Billy's mom was like that. Still, from the way Billy was acting, Tim could tell it was Billy who had put her up to it.

"Here — I'll tell you what," Tito said, putting a comforting arm around Billy's shoulders. "Don DeGeronimo's not here yet — I'll just switch him with you, Billy, and put you two guys together in sixteen."

"Thanks," Billy said with a grateful smile.

"No sweat," said Tito. "Anything I can do, just ask. We aim to please here at Camp Wickasaukee."

"Great," Tim said, with just an edge of annoyance in his voice.

"First year here, huh?"

"Uh-huh," Billy said.

"How many years for you?" Tim asked.

"Seven. Once you get hooked, there's nothing that can keep you away. Hey, you know who else is coming here for the first time this year?"

"No. Who?" Billy asked.

"Dick Dunbar."

"The forward at North Carolina?" Tim asked, his jaw dropping. "Second team All-American?"

"That's the one," Tito confirmed. "He's your other counselor, besides me and Jody."

"Awesome!" Tim said. Not only would he be getting tips from NBA players, but Dick Dunbar was going to be one of his counselors!

There was a sudden commotion by the front door. "That must be him now," Tito said, "judging by the noise level. Yo, Dunbar! That you?"

They went back outside, where a dozen or so kids were mobbing the six-foot-eight-inch Dunbar. Tim knew his face from watching the NCAA tournament on TV. "How cool is this?" he asked, turning to Billy. "Come on, let's say hi."

But there was no way they could get near Dick Dunbar. The other kids had him surrounded and were talking his head off, telling him all about Camp Wickasaukee. Apparently, every one of them had been here for years and years.

Tim felt a sudden, unfamiliar shiver of self-doubt go through him. If these kids had been getting coached every summer of their lives, they were sure to be miles ahead of him at basketball. Back at the playground, Tim had been a star. Would he be nothing but a scrub here?

Tim and Billy unpacked their gear and said hello to some of their bunkmates. There was a friendly kid named Bobby Last, who had to be at least six foot three. Then there was a stocky, pug-nosed, freckle-faced kid by the name of Brian Kelly, who looked them up and down like they were defective goods, and shook hands with a limp handshake.

Tim's favorite right off the bat was Don DeGeronimo, a tall, slim, dark-skinned kid with a sly grin, who actually seemed interested in where they were from and what they were into besides basketball.

All in all, it was a start at making new friends. Tim knew in his heart that if Billy hadn't been there, stuck to him like glue and whining about his video game system, he could have made friends a lot quicker. But he didn't want to make it someone else's fault. After all, Billy couldn't help it. Tim just wished he would let it go and try to get into Camp Wickasaukee the way he himself was doing.

They trooped down to dinner, and Tim got his first look at the girls, whose campus was on the far side of the mess hall. Some of them were really cute. He could tell they were checking the boys out, too, giggling like girls do when they get excited about something. He wondered if the boys and girls here had any activities together, but he didn't want to ask, for fear of looking too interested.

That night, there was a campfire down by the lake. The campers gathered in large circles, by bunkhouse, and there was a bonfire for each group. This is cool, Tim thought, gazing at the fires blazing everywhere in the starlit night. He was starting to like it here already.

"Ow," Billy said, swatting at his bare arm. "This place is swarming with mosquitoes!"

"They're not bothering me," Tim said. "Do you have any repellent?"

"I slathered it on back at the bunk," Billy said mournfully. "But it doesn't help. These things are man-eaters."

"I haven't gotten bit once," Tim said.

"Mosquitoes like me," Billy informed him. "Sweet meat, my mom says."

Great, thought Tim. Billy had found something else to complain about besides his video game system.

The veteran campers were hanging out together, trading stories and bragging about stuff they'd done during the past year — games they'd won, places they'd been, girls they'd dated — and bringing up memories of past summers at Wickasaukee.

Tim tried to listen in, even though he felt left out of their conversation. He figured it was a way to get to know them and pick out which kids might be potential friends. They all seemed to think they were big-cheese athletes. Tim could well believe it about some of them, but others looked like they were just bragging.

They roasted marshmallows and made s'mores with chocolate bars and graham crackers, and then it was time for ghost stories. Glancing over at Billy, Tim could tell he was a little scared, especially since the story was about a killer who searched the forests near Camp Wickasaukee, seeking campers to add to his collection of victims.

It was Tito who was telling the tall tale, and Tim liked the way he really got into it, his dark eyes dancing in the flames from the fire. "They say the victims roam the woods to this day, carrying their severed heads in their hands, bouncing them like basketballs . . ."

"Wooo-oooo . . . ," crooned several veteran campers, providing spooky sound effects to embellish the story. Glancing over at Billy, Tim saw him shudder.

Apparently, someone else had noticed too. That night, just as Tim was drifting off to sleep, he heard the door to his and Billy's room creak open. Dark shadows played on the walls, and he heard at least three campers tiptoe into the small cubicle. One of them seemed to be carrying something round in his hands. Tim kept his eyes half shut, pretending to be asleep. From across the room, he could hear Billy snoring.

The intruders stifled giggles as the kid with the round object dropped it right on Billy's stomach — just as another boy flicked on the room light. All three started yelling, "My head! My head! Aaaaah!"

Billy shot straight up in bed, screaming at the top of his lungs. In his hands, he held a basketball with a wig on it. When he realized what it was, he threw it from him and glared angrily at the three laughing campers who had pulled the prank on him. One was

Brian Kelly, the pug-nosed boy. The others were kids Tim had met only briefly, and he couldn't remember their names at the moment, even though he was wide awake now.

Jody, Tito, and Dick Dunbar all barged into the little room. "What the blazes is going on in here?" Jody yelled.

"Billy boy got scared," Brian said, giggling a piggy-like, snorting laugh.

"My head! My head!" one of the others mimicked, and they all started laughing again. Tim found himself laughing, too, in spite of himself. Billy sure had looked funny, all scared like that, with the bewigged basketball in his outstretched hands, screaming like a two-year-old.

Billy cast him a quick glance, and Tim wiped the smile off his face — but it was too late. He could see the hurt look in Billy's eyes, and he felt a sharp pang of guilt, as if he had been the one who'd pulled the nasty prank.

"Get back in bed, the three of you," Jody ordered the offending campers, and they retreated from the room, still giggling and slapping each other five. "You've got bathroom cleanup duty all week, you hear?" he called after them. Even this punishment didn't seem to ruin their good time.

Dick Dunbar was sitting next to Billy with an arm around his shoulders. "Hey, man, don't sweat it. They're just giving you a hard time 'cause you're the new kid. They'll get tired of picking on you if you show 'em you don't care."

"But I do care," Billy said, his chin trembling. "I wanna go home!"

"Billy," Tim said, "your parents are already in Europe, remember? You can't go home."

"Shut up, traitor," Billy said, giving him that hurt look again.

And Tim did shut up. However babyish Billy was being, what Tim had done was to him far worse. What kind of friend was he, anyway?

**3**

**B**illy didn't say anything to Tim about the incident the next morning — not while they were getting dressed, not while they were making their beds and cleaning their room, not while they were lining up outside for flag salute — not even at mess hall during breakfast.

The morning activity this first full day of camp was basketball, of course. They started out by doing drills on one of the outdoor courts. Jody ran the session, and the first thing he had them all do was run ten laps around the court. By lap number seven, Billy was dragging behind badly, along with one or two other campers who looked equally out of shape.

Tim was pretty winded himself, but he was determined to show the counselors, and most of all, the other campers, that he could keep up with any of them. Midway through lap nine, Billy stopped running altogether and sat down cross-legged on the edge of the court, looking distinctly green.

As Tim came around the court on lap ten, he wanted to stop and ask Billy if he was okay. But he knew if he did, he'd finish way behind the others, with the two other slacker kids. Tim was torn, especially after what had happened last night.

As he came up beside Billy, he saw that his friend was panting hard, staring at the ground. Oh well, thought Tim, he won't notice if I don't stop.

So he kept on going and finished right in the middle of the pack. When they'd all caught their breath, the other kids started hooting and hollering at the three who were still not done — most of all at Billy, who couldn't have cared less.

"Let's go, let's go," Jody urged the three lagging campers, clapping his hands together. "Gotta get in shape, you guys! Gotta keep up!"

Billy and the other two kids finished, collapsing on the ground to more hoots and applause from the others. "Come on, you slackers, get up!" shouted one of them, a slim, athletic-looking blond-haired kid.

"Zip it, Gruber," Jody warned. "Mind your own business."

27

They went on to do some drills — layups from both sides, fast breaks, five-man weaves — with Jody and Dick Dunbar giving coaching pointers along the way. It was Tim's first chance to get a look at the other kids' basketball skills and compare them with his own. He thought he stood up pretty well, but a few kids were way better than him or anyone else — especially Don DeGeronimo and the kid named Gruber.

Of course, they hadn't started shooting from the outside yet — Tim's weakest area. He was dreading the moment he shot his first brick at the hoop.

Billy looked like he was having a miserable time, but Tim tried to keep his distance. He didn't want to be looked at as Billy's nursemaid, first of all. And second, he wasn't sure if Billy was still mad at him over last night's prank.

After drills and a short water break, Jody announced, "Okay, Donnie and Gruber, you two are captains for the scrimmage. Donnie, your team is the Skins. Mike, you're Shirts, and you pick first."

While Donnie removed his shirt, Mike Gruber looked around at the assembled campers, considering whom to pick. "I've got Last," he said, picking the tallest kid of the whole bunch. Donnie picked next, and they took turns until all sixteen campers were picked. Tim was picked twelfth — he guessed because none of them knew how well he could play — and Billy went dead last. Both of them were on the Skins. Tim winced at the sight of Billy's shirtless, flabby frame. Nearly everyone else looked buff by comparison.

The scrimmage began, and Tim watched from the sidelines as the starters went at each other. He was determined to show them all that he deserved to get picked higher than twelfth out of sixteen. He just hoped he got enough playing time to do it.

He could see that some of the kids could really play the game. Well, no wonder, he thought. They've been coming here for, what, seven years? Bob Last was pretty good for a guy his size. He had a nice, soft jump shot, and boy, could he block shots and haul down rebounds. But Donnie, who was maybe two inches shorter, could jump higher and dribble rings around him, and he had amazing moves, not to mention being just as good a shooter.

Mike Gruber, that blond-haired pip-squeak, was amazing at handling the ball. He was even shorter than Tim, but nobody could stop him, not even Donnie.

He played — and shot the ball from the outside — the way Tim wanted to. Tim determined to make friends with Mike Gruber and learn everything he could from him.

Ten minutes into the scrimmage, Jody yelled, "Subs in!" On each team, three kids headed for the sidelines, and the three who'd been standing around went in to replace them. Billy was subbing at center for Don DeGeronimo. Tim went in for the Skins starting point guard, Merrick Jones — an African-American kid with a shaved head whom the other kids called Cue Ball. In fact, every kid here seemed to have a nickname. He wondered what his and Billy's would wind up being.

Despite the fact that he was the Skins point guard now, Tim hardly even got his hands on the ball the whole time he was in the game. He would pass the ball, only to find that it never came back his way. Sometimes, it was because the other kids were hogging it, taking wild, forced shots just to impress everyone. But Tim got the uneasy feeling that some of the time, kids were just passing it to their friends, ignoring the kids they didn't know. All the more reason to make new friends fast, he thought.

Billy actually blocked a shot by Bob Last's replacement — Rich Dauer, one of the three kids who'd pulled the prank the night before — and got a round of applause and amazed laughter, both from his teammates and from the Shirts. There were whispered comments and giggles, but Tim was proud of his buddy. He only wished he had the chance to show the other kids what he could do, too.

Determined to make an impression, Tim decided that if he got the ball again, he was going to make the most of his opportunity. Not two seconds later, he saw an opening. He leaped into the passing lane to steal the ball from one of the Shirts. He raced downcourt, ignoring the shouts of his teammates for him to pass it to them. Two Shirts came over to double-team him, but Tim didn't care. He tried to force his way through and lifted a long jumper that caught nothing but air. He felt his face get red at the sound of the groans he heard, but did his best to ignore them.

Tim touched the ball exactly once more that morning, picking up a loose ball. But instead of passing it upcourt like he normally would have done, he maniacally kept dribbling around the defenders who swarmed him. Before he knew it, the whistle had blown — he'd failed to get the ball up to half-court in time. He'd turned the ball over!

The scrimmage ended with the Shirts ahead 21–17. Nobody came up to Tim afterward to say, "Hey, you're really good," or "Nice game," or anything like that. He found himself walking back to the bunkhouse thinking that he had to improve in a hurry if he was going to meet the standards of Camp Wickasaukee. This place meant business!

"This camp bites," Billy muttered over his tuna casserole — not loud enough to be heard by the rest of the kids, but only by Tim, who was sitting next to him. The seat on Billy's other side was empty. Apparently, none of the other campers had seen fit to sit next to the big, unathletic kid who was scared of mosquitoes and headless campers wandering around in the night.

"Give it a chance, Billy," Tim urged him. "It's just the first full day, man — things are bound to get better."

Billy snorted. "Yeah, I'm sure."

"You'll see, bro. Once they get to know you, they'll see what a great guy you are."

Billy made a face. "This tuna fish tastes like metal,"

he said, shoving it to the far side of his plate with his fork. "Probably full of mercury."

"Billy . . ."

"Man, I could have been in Rome right now, touring the Vatican. Instead, I get basketballs dumped on my stomach at night, and by day, I get to run around till I puke or faint. What a fun experience — not."

"Hey, we both need to get in better shape," Tim said, meaning it.

"I still say this camp bites," Billy said, a little louder this time.

Looking around, Tim saw that Brian Kelly was staring right at them. He could tell at a glance that Brian had overheard Billy. Tim felt a sudden surge of alarm go through him. If Brian Kelly knew, soon everyone in the bunk would know that Billy hated Camp Wickasaukee.

What worried Tim most of all was that they would think he hated it, too. And if they did, what would they do about it?

**4**

The afternoon was hot, and Tim was just as glad as everyone else that they had swimming scheduled next. The campers all dove into the lake to cool off, and were splashing around having a good time when a big, beefcakey guy with a shaved head blew his whistle, and they all stopped where they were.

"Okay," he said. "Hi, everybody. I'm Max. And it's time for you to get certified. Everybody out of the water and onto the dock."

They spent the next hour doing laps, treading water, and hauling their fellow campers out of the lake in rescue exercises.

Tim was tired from the morning of basketball. Midway through his third lap of three, he began to panic, thinking he might go under. He'd never been a great swimmer — sank like a stone if he didn't work really hard to stay afloat — and he thought his arms and legs would give out before he reached the dock. Only through sheer determination did he fight through it and make it to the end of the swimming lane to earn his Shark certification. This meant he was permitted to take out canoes and rowboats and to swim in the deep-water area.

As for Billy, he was deemed a good enough swimmer to earn Whale certification. That meant he could swim anywhere in the lake, as long as he was with a fellow Whale. Tim was glad for his friend. At least Billy was good at something athletic. Maybe he could spend the whole four weeks in the water and avoid the other sports altogether.

After swimming, they had a pickup softball game, just for fun, and then they were given an hour of free time before dinner. "I'm totally exhausted," Tim said, sitting on his bed. "How 'bout you?"

"They'd better give us double portions at dinner," Billy replied, hauling his Camp Wickasaukee T-shirt over his head and throwing it into a corner that would become his laundry pile. "I feel like I've lost ten pounds already."

"Well, there's worse things than getting into shape,"

Tim pointed out as gently as he could. He thought Billy could stand to lose at least twenty, maybe thirty pounds.

"Are you saying I'm fat?"

"No, I just said there are worse things than getting in shape."

"Like what?" Billy asked, collapsing onto his bed. He lay back on his pillow — and let out a howl. "Aaaahhh!" He sprang upright. "What the —?"

He swiped at his head and came up with a handful of shaving cream. "Okay, whose idea of a joke was this?"

Tim had never seen his friend so angry. For a minute, he thought he could see smoke coming out of Billy's ears.

When Billy wasn't looking, Tim felt his own pillow. It was dry — shaving cream–free. Apparently, whoever had it in for Billy was not focusing on Tim. He felt relieved, and ashamed, all at the same time.

"You gonna report it to Jody?" he asked Billy.

"What for?" he asked, wiping his head with a towel. "A lot of good that'd do. He's probably laughing about it with the rest of them right now."

Tim wanted to tell Billy it wasn't true — but what if he was wrong and Billy was right?

Four more days went by — days of nonstop sports and activities. Tim could feel the difference in his stamina, the hardness of the muscles in his legs and stomach, and he knew he was getting into the best shape of his life.

Even Billy was looking less out of shape. His latest problem was sunburned skin — mostly from being on the Skins three times in a row at scrimmages. On the fourth day, Tim noticed that Billy had ducked out of morning drills and snuck down to the lake for extra swimming — with a T-shirt on for sun protection.

The other kids had noticed this, too. They must have thought Billy was too scared to play b-ball anymore, because later that day, when they passed by him, they all started clucking like chickens. Billy didn't do much of anything about it — what could he do except complain? And what good would that have done? It would only have brought more humiliation down on him.

Still, Tim felt he had to do something to help his

friend get over the hump. So when he spotted Jody shaving in the bathroom, he approached him.

"Hey," Jody greeted him, his face half covered in shaving cream. "How's it going?"

Tim wondered if it was the same shaving cream that had wound up on Billy's pillow. Not many of the kids were old enough to be shaving yet. "Okay, I guess," Tim said. "The thing is . . . I'm kind of worried about Billy."

"Yeah? Why's that? Something wrong with him?"

"I . . . well, yeah, he's having a pretty hard time."

"This wouldn't have anything to do with what happened that first night, would it?"

"Uh, yeah, sort of — and he got shaving cream on his pillow, too. Plus, I think he's homesick."

Jody finished shaving with a few quick strokes, toweled off his face, and turned to Tim. "You sure this is about Billy, and not about you?"

Tim was taken aback. "Uh, yeah. Why?"

"Just wondering. You're sure?"

"Sure I'm sure!"

"So everything's cool with you?"

"Yeah."

"Good. Look, Tim," he said, putting an arm around

Tim's shoulders, "sometimes kids have a tough time when they go away from home for the first time, you know? And I know the kids here like to have fun with the 'newbies,' but you've gotta have a sense of humor about it. Your friend Billy'll be okay. Most everybody gets used to camp life after a while — once they decide they're not gonna run home to their mommy and daddy."

"But —"

"If I were you? Just a piece of friendly advice — I'd concentrate on myself. You know, make some new friends here and stop hanging around with just your old friend. He'll be all right — question is, will you?"

"I already told you —"

"Okay, okay," Jody said, backing off. "Just trying to be helpful. Billy needs to get tough a little, if you ask me. I'll keep an eye on him and make sure nothing really serious happens. And you concentrate on you. Deal?"

Jody put his hand out, and Tim reluctantly shook it. "Deal," he said, forcing a smile.

"Good. I'm glad we had this little talk. Hey, once we really get into the swing of things, I'm sure both of you'll forget all about this."

"I thought we already were in the swing of things."

"Oh yeah?" Jody chuckled. "Wait till intercamp games get started."

"Intercamp games?"

"Geez, didn't they tell you anything? We've got our first matchup on Saturday against Camp Weequahic. It'll give you a chance to show everybody what you can do on the court. You look like you can bust some moves, am I right?"

"Uh-huh."

"I thought so. You work hard, you're gonna be a player. Just concentrate on your game and let Billy fend for himself."

"Okay."

"Trust me, he'll be fine."

Tim wanted to say, "You don't know him like I do," but he didn't. He knew it wasn't what Jody wanted to hear, so what was the point? Anyway, Jody was right about one thing — whatever Tim did, when push came to shove, Billy was going to have to make his own way.

**5**

The campers spent the entire next day preparing for the big intercamp match. "Wickasaukee hasn't lost an intercamp games in ten years!" thundered Coach Gabe at morning flag-raising. "And we're not going to lose one this year either!" This was the signal for a rousing cheer and the singing of "Dear Old Wickasaukee."

"This makes me want to puke," Billy murmured under his breath to Tim, who was standing next to him. But Tim made no response. He didn't want to get drawn any further into Billy's war with the camp.

Jody was right, Tim had decided. The problem was in Billy's head, and as long as he kept up the bellyaching, he'd be a natural target for pranks.

They practiced hard for the competition against Camp Weequahic. At basketball, instead of the usual

41

scrimmage, there was no dividing up into teams. The campers were all on the same side, from now till after the games were over. Instead, they mapped out plays for tomorrow's game.

Dick Dunbar was in charge, showing them how it was done down at North Carolina. "This is a pick-and-roll option we call the Brooklyn. In this play, the point guard passes the ball to the center at the top of the key. The center passes to the shooting guard, and at the same time, the point guard makes for the basket without the ball. The shooting guard bounce-passes it down the lane to him, and the point guard goes for the layup. If he misses, both forwards are at the low post, ready for the rebound."

They learned the Chicago, the Miami, and the Buffalo, too. They practiced give-and-gos, pick-and-rolls, five-man weaves, and all kinds of other maneuvers that were new to Tim, let alone to Billy — who was certainly good at setting a pick. Billy pretty much flattened Mike Gruber when he tried to get through him on defense.

"Man, what are you, an oak tree?" Gruber complained. And for today, at least, Billy's nickname was

Oak Man. It was a welcome change, and Tim even thought he saw Billy smile once or twice.

When Saturday morning came, the green Weequahic buses pulled up for the games. "Man, they look like a buncha wusses!" Brian Kelly snorted as the visitors piled out of the buses and were organized in the parking lot by age groups.

"This is gonna be cake," said Bobby Last, high fiving his best friend, Derek Chang. "No sweat."

Tim felt his heart swell with confidence. It was nice to be part of a team that felt like a winner — even if they hadn't done anything yet to deserve it.

The games commenced. Since there were sixteen kids in the Eagles group, and only two hours before lunch and three after, not everyone could play in every sport. Each camper got to be in three events. Tim looked over his assignments and was pleased to see that he was on the team for the big afternoon basketball game. He was also set for softball and the 100-yard dash. "What'd you get?" he asked Billy.

"Swimming."

"Cool. That's good, Billy."

Billy shot him a look. "Yeah, I guess. I also got tennis and softball."

"Hey, we're on a team together!" Tim said, patting his friend on the back.

"Yay," Billy said, a little overenthusiastically. "We can warm the bench together. Whoopee!"

There were several events going on at once, all around the camp. Basketball, being the featured sport, counted for twice as many points as anything else. The first events of the morning got under way. Billy went down to the lake while Tim got set for his 100-yard dash.

He took his position at the starting line alongside several other runners. The pistol sounded, and Tim took off in a blur of motion. His legs fired like pistons, and he carried his momentum forward until he broke the string at the finish line. Looking over his shoulder, he saw that he had beaten the others by a good six feet — a wide margin for such a short race. He heard cheers all around him, and his name was shouted in triumph. He raised a fist in the air as he trotted back to the sidelines and accepted the hearty backslaps and high-fives of his campmates.

At lunch, the kids shared stories of their morning

exploits. While there had been no official announcement of the score, Tito quietly let it be known that Wickasaukee had a comfortable lead. Feelings were warm and comradely in the mess hall. Outside, they could see the Weequahic campers picnicking glumly on the grass, with the hot sun beating mercilessly down on them.

"How'd you do in swimming?" Tim asked Billy, who actually smiled — beamed, in fact — as he answered by holding up his index finger.

"First place?" Tim asked.

"In three separate races," Billy confirmed.

"Dude, that's awesome. You rule!" Tim said, slapping his friend on the back.

"Yeah, right. I'm the king of Wickasaukee," Billy said sarcastically.

"Didn't anybody congratulate you?" Tim asked.

"Yeah, man," Billy said. "I'm okay with them for now, but you'll see — soon it'll be 'What have you done for me lately?' "

Tim shook his head and sighed. Jody was right, he decided. Billy was just taking it all the wrong way.

After lunch, they had their softball game. Billy actually started the game at catcher but came out after three error-prone innings. Tim went in during the fourth inning and had a walk and a double while scoring two runs in a 6–4 Wickasaukee victory.

"This is too easy, man," Tim heard Brian Kelly say to Mike Gruber. "Let's have some fun with these losers on the basketball court."

The game started at 4 P.M., right after a 46–32 victory for the Wickasaukee Condors. All the other events of the day were now completed, so the entire boys camp was in the bleacher seats on each side of the gym to watch the Eagles complete the day's triumph. Apparently, the girls were having a similar event over on their side of the camp — although they didn't have a ten-year string of victories to defend.

The ref blew his whistle, and Jody, their coach for the game, gathered the team members around him. "Donnie and Derek, you start at forward. Gruber and Cue Ball, you're the guards. Last at center. The rest of you, I'll get you in there, don't worry. Soon as we build up a cushion."

By halftime, the Eagles had a 20-point lead, and Tim was sent out for the second half, along with the other subs. He felt kind of off, going in like this with a big lead. It was kind of a no-win situation. If they piled it on, it was no big deal — the game had already essentially been won. If they blew the lead even a little bit, they'd look like scrubs. And as the point guard, and Mike Gruber's replacement, that went double for him. Gruber had been the big star of the first half, sinking four 3-pointers and setting the tone for the game.

Tim started out by running the plays Dick Dunbar had shown them — the Brooklyn, the Chicago, the Buffalo — but the guys on the court with him weren't nearly as good as the starters Gruber had. They dropped his passes, or mistimed their moves so that he looked like he was passing to nowhere. Then, when Tim decided to scrap the plays and get back to playground ball — meaning taking over the game — he blew his dribble twice and threw three bricks that clanged off the backboard without even hitting the rim. Man, did he ever need to work on his jumper.

The Weequahic team closed to within 12 points, and Jody called for a time-out to switch back to his starters. Tim rode the bench for the rest of the game, which ended in a 32-point victory for the Eagles. He sat there, glum, throughout the celebration afterward. Even when Coach Gabe took the microphone to

47

announce that Wickasaukee had won the games by a score of 105–35, Tim couldn't muster up more than a halfhearted cheer, while everyone around him exploded in shouts of victory.

Sure, he'd done well in track and softball. But everyone had done well all day long. And when he'd gotten his first big chance to show what he could do on the basketball court, he'd blown it big-time.

Would he even get a second chance to prove himself?

**6**

few more days went by, and all anyone was talking about was the upcoming social — the first dance of the summer. For the new campers, like Tim, it was their first chance to get a look at the girls up close. Girls had always made Tim nervous. He had had all kinds of crushes, since he was in second grade, but he'd never really asked a girl to dance. And with camp socials, it turned out, that was pretty much the whole trick.

The campers who had been here year after year, of course, already had a pretty good idea of how things went. They knew which girls were going with which boys the summer before, and a lot of the talk was to sound each other out about whom it was okay to ask to dance. "What about Rise Lawrence?" Brian Kelly was asking the group of boys sitting on the front steps of Eagles Nest. "Who's she with?"

"I heard she likes Donnie," said Bobby Last. "She's tall, y'know? Tall girls like tall guys."

"Like you?" teased Mike Gruber. "When did you ever go with her?"

"I didn't say I did," Bobby said defensively.

"'Tall girls like tall guys,'" Gruber mocked.

"Shut up, shorty," Bobby said, and gave Gruber a halfhearted shove. All the boys laughed. Tim noticed that Mike didn't seem to mind being called shorty. If it had been him, he wouldn't have been able to take it so well. That was what made Mike Gruber so cool. He seemed not to care about anything — except basketball, of course.

They talked about Rise Lawrence and Joanie Kim and Stephanie Krause. Rating them against each other. Tim felt awful when they did that, especially when they dissed kids because of their looks, or the way they walked, or their weird voice, or whatever it was. It was the same way they ragged on the new campers — although Tim doubted they'd have had the guts to say those things to the girls' faces the way they did with the other boys.

He wanted to hang with these kids, to feel free and easy with them. He guessed it would come with time, but he didn't want to force it — didn't want to sit down there with them and talk people down just to feel bigger.

So he went back inside and upstairs to his and Billy's room. Billy was lying on his bed, reading a long letter from Europe. "So how're your mom and dad liking their trip?" Tim asked him.

"A lot better than I'm liking it here," Billy said miserably. "You should read this — they've been to about six hundred places already, and all my mom does is rave about how great it all is. I can't believe they didn't take me!"

"You really like going to old churches and stuff?" Tim asked.

"It sure beats getting made fun of, being bitten by a million bugs, getting your head covered with shaving cream, and peeling the skin off your back in huge sheets," Billy replied. "I'm gonna look ridiculous tonight."

"Nobody will notice that you're peeling," Tim said. "Just wear a shirt."

"Thanks. I was planning on it."

51

"Good. No, but seriously, you look okay. A little red is all. Lots of guys have sunburns from this week. It hasn't rained once yet."

"I hate dancing," Billy said. "I'm no good at it."

"Look, all you have to do is dance one dance with a girl, then ask her if she wants to go outside and talk."

"Oh, so you've got all the moves down now?" Billy said, looking doubtful. "Where'd you get that info?"

"Listening to the other guys talk about it," Tim admitted. "But I'm sure you can dance as well as anybody else."

"I wouldn't know," Billy said glumly. "I've never tried."

"Never?"

"Never."

"Ah, it's nothing to worry about, dude," Tim assured him. "It's just a dance." Tim flopped down on his own bed, wishing someone else were giving him a pep talk, instead of the other way around.

The gym was all strung up with Christmas lights, even though it was July. Independence Day was the only holiday of the summer, and the camp was taking full advantage of it. Tonight, after the social, there would be a display of fireworks down by the lake.

Tim looked around at the flickering lights, topped off by a rotating mirror ball and disco lights. On his side of the gym, all the boys from age eleven on up were hanging together in groups, checking out the girls, who were doing the same thing on the other side. Everyone was dressed up, which, here at Wickasaukee, meant that the guys had showered, moussed their hair, and were wearing slacks instead of jeans or shorts and regular shoes instead of sneakers. The girls were all decked out in dresses, heels, and makeup. It kind of gave Tim the willies. "No pressure," he told himself under his breath, but he couldn't deny he was feeling it. Most of the boys were, by the looks of them.

The music was already playing, courtesy of a DJ who was parked on the stage, surrounded by his equipment. A lot of the Condors were up and dancing already with the girl Condors. Some of the counselors were serving punch and cookies at the other end of the gym.

Tim wondered which of the Eagles would be the first of their group to break the ice by asking someone to dance. Would it be a girl Eagle, or would one of the boys step forward first, cross that dance floor with every eye in the place on him, and tap the girl of his choice on the shoulder?

Don DeGeronimo was on his feet, being gently shoved forward by Tito, who wore a sneaky grin on his face. Don went straight across the gym floor, bopping to the music, looking molto casual, and sidled up to Rise Lawrence, a tall blond-haired girl with huge blue eyes. Donnie tapped her on the shoulder, and she put her hand to her chest as if to say, "Me?" Donnie nodded, she smiled, and the two of them walked out onto the floor together to dance.

"Way to go, Donnie!" Brian Kelly said, high fiving the kids nearest him.

Big shot, Tim said to himself. Let's see you go ask somebody.

Tim started checking out the girls to see whom he might ask. His eye rested on a girl with shiny black hair cascading down her back — a girl with twinkling dark eyes and a dazzling smile. He wondered what her name was — if she was one of the girls the boys had been talking about. Maybe she was new here, and he had as good a chance as anybody else.

"Come on, you losers!" Tito was saying, goading them on. "What are you afraid of? A bunch of girls? Get out there and ask somebody to dance!"

"How come they don't have to ask us?" Merrick asked.

"Quit squealing and get out there, Cue Ball," Tito insisted, ignoring the question. But Tim *did* wish it was that way. Having to make the first move was hard. And after all, whose law was it that guys had to do the asking?

"Well, Daniels?" Tito came up to him from behind. "Time's a-wasting. Not scared, are you?"

"Me? No way!" Tim said, feeling instantly terrified. He only wondered how Billy would react when Tito got to him. He glanced around to see where Billy was and found him cowering by the corner of the bleachers, a look of utter dread on his face.

Tim launched himself across the floor, which was filling by now with couples dancing. He looked for the black-haired girl but didn't see her. Where had she gone? He'd only turned his head away for a few seconds!

There she was — on the dance floor, kickin' it live with Mike Gruber. Argh! AAARGH!

He knew this feeling — knew it from second grade, and then again in fifth, and yet again in sixth. He had a crush.

He didn't even know this girl's name. He'd never even talked to her. He knew not one thing about her, except that her hair was black and her eyes were twinkly and her smile was, well, perfect. But the minute he'd seen her dancing with Mike Gruber, he knew.

Suddenly he realized he was standing right next to a knot of girls who were waiting to get asked to dance. They were whispering to each other and giggling and checking out the boys out of the corners of their eyes. Tim was seized by a sudden resolve not to let anyone know what he was feeling. Not to let anyone know he had a crush on . . . whatever her name was.

He stepped up to a cute, kind of chubby, freckle-faced girl and said, "Wanna dance?"

"Sure," she replied, smiling and showing a mouthful of braces. "I'm Wanda. What's your name?"

"Tim. Tim Daniels."

"Cute name!" she said, giggling as he took her hand and led her out onto the floor. They danced a little, and now and then, Tim snuck a look over at Mike

Gruber and his dancing partner. He tried to maneuver himself and Wanda closer to them, until they were close enough for him to wave at Mike and say hi.

Mike grinned and gave him the high sign, as if to say, "Good work, pal, you picked a real winner." Tim thought Wanda was okay for sure. But he couldn't take his eyes off the black-haired girl. Except when she happened to catch him at it — or almost catch him. Tim wasn't sure which, but either way, he looked away in a hurry. When he looked back, she was whispering to Mike and giggling, casting quick glances at him. Yep, he guessed she'd caught him staring. Great. Just great.

Maybe she was giggling at him because she thought he was cute. Nah, thought Tim, it couldn't be that. Probably Mike Gruber was telling her stuff about him, and making him look like an idiot in her eyes. All the mistakes he'd made playing b-ball, all about Tim being best friends with Billy Futterman the geek.

The word made Tim wince. He'd never called anybody a geek in his life, but he could easily picture Mike Gruber doing it. He was probably calling Tim a geek right now — that would explain the girl's giggling. . . .

"You okay?" Wanda asked suddenly.

"Uh, yeah," Tim said hurriedly. "Why?"

"You stopped moving."

"Huh?"

"You're just, like, standing there. Sure you're okay?"

"Yeah, I'm just . . . thirsty. Yeah, that's it. Wanna get something to drink?"

"Sure."

She followed him over to the punch table, and they kind of stood around for a while, sipping punch and nibbling on cookies, checking out all the rest of the kids.

And then he saw her coming toward him. He had to get away — now. His stomach was heaving, and he was afraid he was going to be sick right there in front of everybody. "Hi," she said, in a voice like liquid silver. "I'm Stephanie. You, um, wanna dance?"

Tim froze, his jaw working but no words coming out. "I . . . uh . . . um . . ." He looked over at Wanda. She was pretending not to notice him and Stephanie, but Tim could tell she noticed, all right. She'd probably feel hurt if he said yes — but how could he not? She'd asked him, for goodness' sake! "Uh, sure," he said, then turned to Wanda and said, "See you later, okay?"

Wanda flashed a quick smile and waved, turning her back to him as he followed Stephanie out onto the floor. She was taller than he was, by a good three inches, but he didn't care. He just hoped she didn't.

They danced for a while to a hip-hop number, Tim's heart pounding as he felt the eyes of everyone in the room on the two of them. He couldn't believe it — one of the prettiest girls in the whole place had asked him to dance. It meant she must like him better than Mike Gruber!

The DJ lowered the lights. "Okay, everyone," he said over the microphone, "it's time for some slow dancing. Grab your partners and cuddle up close."

She was looking straight at him with those twinkling eyes of hers, but he couldn't hold her gaze. Looking at the ground, he reached out and drew her closer, into slow-dancing position. They rocked around the floor to some song he didn't even hear, spinning slowly. Every few seconds, he looked up at Stephanie's black hair — or worse, straight into her twinkling eyes — and quickly looked away.

Her perfume was sweet but strong. Suddenly, he could barely breathe — the smell of it was making him dizzy . . . he was going to be sick for sure, if he didn't leave the gym pronto. "I . . . excuse me," he told Stephanie, backing away.

"You okay?" she asked, concerned.

"Yeah, it's just . . . I'll be right back."

He threaded his way through the couples on the floor and headed for the far side doors, which were half hidden in darkness. Behind him, he could feel a hundred pairs of eyes watching him beat a shameful retreat. He banged the door open and stood outside on the porch, breathing in huge gulps of the fresh mountain air. Overhead, the moon shone brightly. Billions of crickets chirped, and the throbbing sound of music from inside mingled with nature's orchestra.

Tim turned and looked back in through one of the windows. He could see Stephanie, surrounded by a bunch of girls, all of them giggling and casting glances toward the door he'd exited. Making fun of him, no doubt. How could he have ever thought she liked him — him, a new camper who wasn't even all that good at basketball, and who had a nerdy friend, and didn't know how to act around girls he liked.

Why would she ever like him? Why would anybody?

Now he knew just how Billy had been feeling all this time. Made fun of wherever he went. Later, back at the bunkhouse, he'd be sure to apologize to Billy for joining in the torment, even if he'd only done it a little bit.

He spent the rest of the dance out on the porch, except for once or twice when he went in and asked Wanda to dance. She was nice, she was comfortable, not bad-looking, and she didn't make him the least bit nervous. Too bad he didn't have a crush on her. And too bad Stephanie thought he was ridiculous.

He walked back to the bunkhouse a good way behind the other campers in his group. He was busy trying to frame an apology to Billy. But he never got the chance to give it, because when he climbed the stairs and threw open the door of their room, Billy was already in a screaming, froth-at-the-mouth rage.

"Will you look at this?" he shrieked. "Look. Just look!" He pointed to his bed. Tim went over to it and peeled back the blanket. Someone had short-sheeted the bed and slit the sheet, so that when Billy had gotten into bed, he'd ripped it right in half!

**7**

**A**ll right, everybody out of bed — now!" Jody was steaming mad, no doubt about it. "I've had about enough of this, okay? Now every last one of you is gonna contribute one dollar to the Billy Futterman buy-a-sheet fund. Then you're gonna make his bed with new sheets — and you're gonna make it perfectly, do you understand?"

There were some mumbled replies from the chastened campers. "I can't hear you!" Jody shouted.

"Yes!" they all responded in unison.

"Yes what?"

"Yes, we understand!"

"You'd better. Now, let's go. I'm gonna drop a dime on that blanket when you're done, and it better bounce back!"

The Eagles went into action, throwing dirty looks at

Billy Futterman as they worked on his bed, yanking the sheets back and forth and tucking them in tightly.

Billy didn't seem to care. He was allowing himself to enjoy this brief moment of payback, and he stood there, his arms folded, a satisfied smile on his face.

Tim thought he was making a big mistake. The kids were only going to hold a grudge against him. If Billy thought the worst was over because he'd told Jody on them, he was way wrong.

Sure enough, the next morning, when the whole camp had assembled for flag raising, Coach Gabe looked up at the top of the flagpole and froze.

"What is that up there?" he asked, even though he knew full well what it was. "Is that someone's underwear?" He hauled it down and read the nametag inside. "Billy Futterman — I believe these are yours . . . ," he said, holding them up with two fingers at arm's length, like they smelled or something. "Would you please come up here and get them?"

Billy shambled forward, to the hoots and laughter of the assembled campers, and retrieved his pilfered boxers. His face was as red as cranberries, and Tim could see the tears of shame glistening on his cheeks. He felt painfully sad for his friend's agony. But at the same time, he was as glad as could be that it wasn't his underwear.

"Hey, Tim!"

Tim looked up from his arts-and-crafts project to see Tito coming toward him, a smile on his face. "Hey."

"Whatcha got there?" Tito asked, looking at Tim's piece of sculpture.

"It's gonna be a candy dish," Tim explained, cocking his head sideways to try to see a candy dish in the unformed lump of clay he'd been working on since lunch. All day long, the Eagles had been relegated to indoor activities as punishment for hoisting Billy's Skivvies up the flagpole. A full day of arts and crafts, bunk cleaning, and nap time had made everyone antsy and grouchy.

But Tito seemed in good spirits. "I need you to go down to Max at the lake and get me the jetty scraper, okay?"

"Okay," said Tim. He got up, stretched, and went outside into the blinding sunlight.

It was a long walk down to the lake. "Hi, Max," he

64

greeted the swim counselor. "Tito told me to ask you for his jetty scraper."

"The jetty scraper?" Max repeated, scratching his head. "Oh, yeah — I loaned it to Fred Ferguson. Go ask him for it."

Fred Ferguson was the tennis coach, and the tennis courts were way back on the other side of the camp. But what choice did Tim have? He didn't want to come back to Tito empty-handed. So he crossed the whole campus to the tennis courts and found Fred Ferguson giving a group lesson.

"The jetty scraper . . . hmmm . . . who did I lend that to? Oh, yeah — the chef has it over at the mess hall. He's probably done with it by now. Why don't you ask him for it?"

Tim sighed in growing exasperation — the mess hall was way back the other way, past the swimming area. So he crossed the whole campus yet again — and when he got there, the chef wasn't even there. Rory, the assistant cook, told him the chef was in his bunk, taking a nap between making meals. So Tim had to climb the hill to the very top, where he roused the chef, and asked once again for the jetty scraper.

"Oh, wait . . . I left it at the mess hall, with Rory. Go ask him."

This was getting really frustrating. Tim headed back down the hill and asked Rory for the scraper. "Jody wanted to borrow it this morning," Rory said. "So I loaned it to him."

"But it wasn't yours to lend!" Tim said, exasperated. "It was Tito's."

"Oh. Yeah. True. Well, he probably has it back by now."

Tim went looking for Jody and found him lying in his bed, reading a magazine on his free hour. "The jetty scraper?" he asked. "I think I left it by the front steps. Check around there."

Tim wanted to ask what it looked like, since he'd never actually seen a jetty scraper before. In fact, he'd never even heard of one till now. But he didn't want to look like a jerk, so he left Jody without asking him.

Coming down the front steps, he was about to start looking around for it — whatever it was. Instead, he saw Billy doing just that. "Looking for the jetty scraper?" Tim asked.

"Huh? No, the sky hook," Billy replied. "I've been

going around all over the place trying to track it down for Tito."

"Wait a minute," Tim said, sitting down on the steps. "Wait just a doggone minute!"

"What?" Billy asked.

"I have a funny feeling we've been had."

"What do you mean?"

"Ever hear of a wild goose chase, Billy?"

"Sure."

"I think we've just been on one."

From inside the arts-and-crafts hut, they could hear the sound of laughter. Tito's head popped out the window overhead. "Find that jetty scraper yet?" he asked, cracking a sly grin.

That night as the two of them lay awake in bed, they heard the door open, creaking softly. Tim wondered what prank was about to be pulled this time, and by whom. But the huge silhouette outlined in the doorway could only have been Dick Dunbar.

"You guys awake?" he asked gently.

"Uh-huh."

"Yeah."

"Can I come in?" He didn't wait for an answer, but instead came into the room, found a chair in the dim light, and sat down between their two beds. "How you guys been doin'?" he asked. "I, um, heard about the little episode today."

"It wasn't so little," Billy said. "And it wasn't the first time, or the second, or the third."

Tim remained silent, content to let Billy do the complaining for him. But he felt awful, knowing that now he was as much the target for the practical jokers as Billy was — and now, even their counselors were in on it!

"That was wrong, what they did to you today," he said. "I just thought you ought to know, they did it to me, too."

"You?"

"Apparently they do it to all the new guys — it's a time-honored Wickasaukee ritual."

"Yeah, right," said Billy. "Why not human sacrifice? That's a time-honored ritual, too."

"Now, come on, Bill," Dunbar said, patting him on the knee. "Cool down. You're still all in one piece. And you know what they say about sticks and stones."

"I don't care," Billy said. "I want to get even. Better than even."

"I don't think that's such a good idea, man," Dick advised.

"Who cares?" Billy said, defiant.

"Look, I know what they've been doing isn't right," the counselor said soothingly, "and it's way over the top, for sure. But trust me, you just hang in there another couple days, and they'll totally drop it."

"Yeah, right."

"No, really — the big thing is not to react. That's only giving those kids what they want — entertainment."

"Kids and counselors," Tim reminded him.

"Yeah, well, I spoke to Jody and Tito about that," Dunbar said. "I think I got through to them some." He got up and went to the door. "Sleep tight, guys. Don't worry — I'll make sure it's a quiet night for you."

"How'll you do that?" Tim asked.

"I'm pulling my cot right out here into the hall." Dunbar waved and softly closed the door behind him.

"Nice guy," Tim said after Dick had left.

"Yeah. The only one, as far as I can see. But that's

okay — I'm gonna get my own back, you wait and see."

"Billy, didn't you hear one word he said?"

"I heard him. I just don't care. And neither should you. Are you with me on this, or not?"

Tim bit his lip and hesitated. "I guess not," he said.

"Fine."

"Billy —"

"I said FINE!"

And those were the last words either of them spoke that night.

"kay, Eagles," Jody said to his campers, who sat grouped around him. "Tomorrow's the big one. Chickasaw was the last camp to beat us in intercamp games — eleven years ago — and they've had it in for us ever since. They're 2–0 going in, we're only 1–0, so they've got more confidence and experience under their belts. I'm telling you, it's going to be a tough day if each and every one of you doesn't do his ultimate best. You understand?"

"Yeah!" everyone shouted together. Even Billy shouted, although Tim knew his heart wasn't in it. Not shouting would've been a bad idea. Next thing you knew, they'd be calling you traitor and treating you like one.

"Now I wanna see some of that spirit in today's scrimmage," Jody said, passing the basketball to Don

DeGeronimo. "You and Gruber choose up, and let's get to it."

Tim found himself on Donnie's team — chosen eleventh — and around midway through the scrimmage came in as a sub, with the assignment of guarding Mike Gruber, who was scoring points all over the place as his Shirts led 14–12.

Tim decided that he would take Jody at his word and play with everything he had. There was no way he would let Mike score off him. Not if he had to foul out trying.

He went for the ball and made Mike turn it over. Gruber glared at him and pointed a silent finger Tim's way. "What?" Tim asked, confused. "What'd I do?"

Next time down the court, Gruber went right at him. Tim held his ground, and the whistle sounded. "Offensive foul. Charging!" Tito called out, giving the ball to Tim to inbound.

Now Mike Gruber looked really mad. Tim enjoyed the moment — he'd played good enough defense to annoy the Eagles starting point guard — and showed the counselors that he could be trusted in a big game, at least on defense.

Mike Gruber was defending him now, and Tim

backed in toward the basket. He was hoping the big guys — Bobby Last and Brian Kelly — would close in on him, and he could then dish it out to one of his teammates for an easy jump shot. The thing was, Mike Gruber kept bumping him and elbowing him. Every time the ref looked away for a moment, he felt another jab in his back.

"Cut it out!" Tim said through clenched teeth.

"Make me," Gruber muttered back, jabbing him in the back even harder.

Tim dished the ball off, turned around, and gave Mike a little shove. Gruber reacted as if he'd been hit by a truck — he staggered backward, his arms waving, and crashed to the gym floor. The whistle blew, and Tito pointed to Tim.

"Flagrant foul," he called. "Two shots plus possession. One more like that and you're out of the game, Daniels!"

"But —"

Tim stopped, knowing it would be no use to complain. Most referees were more interested in establishing that they were in charge than in the fairness of their calls, and Tito was certainly no different.

Gruber sank both foul shots, then inbounded the

ball to Bobby Last. Last drove the lane and slam-dunked it over Donnie D., and the Shirts won the game 21–19. All because Tim had been whistled for a flagrant foul!

His teammates avoided his gaze as he headed for the bleachers at the side of the gym. "Hey, Daniels," Jody said, coming over to him. "You'd better stay away from dumb fouls like that tomorrow against Chicka-saw, or you're liable to cost us a big game."

What about the great "D" I played on Gruber? he wanted to say. Doesn't that count for anything?

But once again, he said nothing. He knew it wouldn't matter. All that mattered was how he played tomorrow.

That night, Tim lay in bed, listening to Billy snore, thinking about the next day's big intercamp games. He wondered how he would do if he'd finally get a chance to impress the kids who mattered here. And more than anything, he wondered about Mike Gruber. Why had he been so mad at Tim? Was it just because Tim had messed him up by playing good defense?

Mike was a pretty intense competitor, and Jody's words had fired everybody else up, too. But Tim couldn't help feeling there was something else behind Mike's hostility, something more personal. Tim wondered if it was about Stephanie Krause. The way she'd asked him to dance at the social . . .

Could it be that Stephanie actually liked him, and that Mike Gruber was jealous? Tim had trouble believing it. Mike was a better athlete than he was, and more to the point, he was cooler, more sure of himself, and much more popular. So why would Stephanie like him over Mike?

Even if she did, Tim decided, he wasn't going to dance with her at the next social. She made him too nervous anyway. Her perfume had got to him so bad that he'd almost lost his cookies. Besides, he didn't need to make an enemy of the second most popular kid in the whole Eagles group.

Tim made up his mind. He wouldn't dance with anyone at the next social. He didn't want Stephanie to think he liked another girl better than her. He'd just avoid dancing altogether.

The battle against Camp Chickasaw did not begin well. The morning's events were a disaster, especially track and swimming, and even in basketball, among the younger groups, Wickasaukee was having trouble holding its own. The word went around at lunchtime that Chickasaw was actually in the lead. It made for some pretty worried faces in the mess hall.

By three o'clock, Tito and Jody were in foul moods. Obviously, they'd heard the results from around the camp, but neither of them would say what the score was. All Jody told them was, "You guys had better win this b-ball game, you got it? The whole camp is counting on you."

It didn't take a genius to get the message. Wickasaukee needed them to win, or the incredible winning streak would be over — and if that happened, it would be all their fault.

"Pssst!" Merrick Jones whispered to them as they stood in their huddle. "The Condors lost their game. If we don't win, Wickasaukee loses."

So that made it official. They put their hands together as one and gave a shout before the starters headed to center court for the opening jump. The subs remained standing in front of their bench, whooping and hollering, cheering their teammates on.

Camp Chickasaw had a center who made Bobby

Last look short. "Geez," Jody muttered under his breath. "That kid's gotta be sixteen at least!"

Chickasaw won the tip-off, thanks to their giant in the middle, who proceeded to open the scoring with a slam dunk. "Hey, Goliath," Mike Gruber yelled at him. "Watch out for my slingshot!"

"Huh?" the giant said dumbly, not getting it.

"Eat this!" Gruber said, driving around him and laying the ball up perfectly to tie the score.

It was a good beginning, but it was the last time Gruber scored in the game. Chickasaw put a guard on him who was just as quick as Mike but a good three inches taller, and Gruber just couldn't seem to get free. The game stayed close until late in the second half, with neither team able to pull away decisively.

Tim got in for a few minutes in the first half and did a passable job. The Eagles were down 5 points when he went in, and down by 3 when Gruber came back into the game for him right before halftime.

With two minutes left in the game, Tim got a second chance to make the difference to his team. On a drive by Chickasaw's point guard, Gruber committed his fifth foul, fouling out of the game. "Daniels, it's up to you," Jody said, grabbing him by both shoulders before shoving him onto the court. "Get out there and nail this game for us!"

Tim felt a chill run up and down his neck. His shoulder blades twitched, and a cold sweat broke out on his forehead as the ref handed him the ball to inbound. Wickasaukee was down by 2 points, with the entire intercamp games riding in the balance.

Why was his mouth suddenly so dry? He could hear his heartbeat drumming in his ears, so loud that it practically drowned everything else out — the roar of the crowd cheering him on, the screaming of both coaches, the pounding of dozens of feet on the wooden bleachers.

Tim's hands felt like two slabs of dead meat. He tried to dribble downcourt but lost control, and the ball bounced right into the hands of the kid guarding him. Before he knew what had happened, the Eagles were down by 4!

Once again Tim brought the ball downcourt, trying with every ounce of his strength to control his nerves. Seeing an open shot, he took it — but he rushed the shot, and the ball clanged off the rim. Luckily, Bobby Last got the rebound and slammed it home. But on their next trip up the court, Tim got tangled up in his own feet and turned the ball over again! Another fast break, and the Eagles were down by 4 again.

Tim drove the lane, desperate now to score. He threw up a layup, only to have it stuffed by Chickasaw's giant center! The ref's whistle blew. "Jump ball!"

It was a joke — the guy was a foot taller than Tim — but somehow, the giant tapped it the wrong way, and Donnie DeGeronimo grabbed the ball and put down a layup. Then, down at the other end, Donnie stuffed a shot by Chickasaw's small forward, and Tim picked up the loose ball.

He knew time was running out. He knew they needed 2 points. He drove to the basket again, determined to score, or to draw the foul. As he jumped, the giant came at him looking for the block. Tim turned in midair, and the giant's arm came down smack on his head.

Tim saw stars for a few seconds, but he'd also heard the whistle blow. He'd drawn the foul, with only one second left in the game. All he had to do now was sink both shots, and Wickasaukee would tie the game, sending it into overtime, where, as the home team, they'd have a big advantage.

Tim tried to quiet his pounding heart, but it just wouldn't stop. He swallowed hard and threw the first foul shot. It clanged on the rim, bounced straight up — and straight back down into the net. A huge cheer went up from the sidelines.

Time for the big one. Tim took the ball from the ref, closed his eyes, and said a silent prayer. Then he opened his eyes and launched the shot. It rose in a beautiful, high arc — and fell a good two feet short of the rim. Airball!

The whistle blew, and the game was over. A stunned silence filled the gym as the Chickasaw campers screamed in triumph. "We won!" they shouted. "We beat Wickasaukee. Who's number one now? We are! Yahoo!"

Tim stood there frozen, gasping for breath, looking at the gym floor between his feet. He could feel the angry, disappointed looks of his fellow campers. Camp Wickasaukee had gone down to its first defeat in ten years, and he — Tim Daniels — was the main reason.

In a horrible, clear moment, Tim saw his future as clear as crystal. From now on, he, not Billy Futterman, would be the most unpopular kid in camp!

The mess hall was deathly quiet that night at supper. Tim could hear the clinking of ice water as it was poured into glasses from pitchers, the clinking of forks and knives on plates, the chewing, but no talking. Tim covered his ears to protect himself from the deafening silence of the huge hall, but it was no use. Everyone at his table kept sneaking hard glances at him, thinking poisonous thoughts.

"Well, look at it this way," Jody said, taking in the whole group of them. "It had to happen sooner or later. No streak lasts forever."

"It didn't have to die today," Mike Gruber muttered under his breath.

"What? You say something?" Jody demanded.

Gruber made a face, shook his head. "Nothin'," he

said, crossing his arms over his chest and looking Tim right in the eyes.

"Come on, man," Donnie DeGeronimo said, shaking Gruber to get him out of his black mood. "It's everybody's fault, not just one person's. We all made mistakes today."

"Only one person made the last mistake — the one that cost us the whole match!"

Tim fought back tears. He was not going to give them the satisfaction of seeing him cry.

"I'm . . . not feeling well," he told Jody. "Could I go back to the bunk and lie down?"

"Uh . . . sure, sure," Jody said. "You wanna go to the infirmary?"

"Nah. I'll be okay. Just . . . could I?"

"Sure. Go lie down and rest." Jody turned a scowl on the other kids. "Now you guys look Tim in the eye and say you're sorry. Say, 'We're all responsible.' Because that's the truth." He paused, but no one spoke up. "Say it!" he repeated. "Gruber, you first."

Mike Gruber turned a look of pure hatred on Tim and said, "I'm sorry, Tim. We're all responsible." Then, one by one, they all said it after him, exactly the same way — and as sincere as the grin on a crocodile.

It didn't make Tim feel any better, though that was clearly what Jody intended. In fact, Tim felt worse — poor him, the baby, who needed the counselor to protect him.

He was almost back to Eagles Nest when Billy caught up to him. Billy was panting, having obviously run all the way. "Hey!" he said. "You okay?"

"Fine," Tim said, not breaking stride.

Billy kept up his quick pace. "That Gruber's a punk," he said.

"Yeah, so?"

"It wasn't your fault we lost."

"It wasn't?" Tim stopped at the front steps and faced his friend. "Sure looked to me like it was."

"Donnie was right. Everybody could've done better. And Jody was right, too — all streaks come to an end. It's a mathematical certainty."

"Ugh." Tim sighed in exasperation. "Why did you follow me here?"

"I just wanted to, you know, stand by you. You're my friend, so —"

"So you attach yourself to me like a puppy dog?" Tim blurted out. "They're right, okay? I'm a loser — and so are you!"

Instantly, he wished he hadn't said it. He realized for the first time how angry he'd been at Billy all this time, for preventing him from being popular here at camp.

"Nice to know you feel that way," Billy said, his lip trembling.

"Oh, come on, I don't really," Tim said, trying to laugh it off. "I don't know why I even said that."

"You said it because it's true," Billy replied, looking right through him.

"It isn't."

"Yes it is, or it wouldn't have been in your mind like that," Billy insisted.

"Billy —"

But Billy was gone, up the stairs and inside the building. Tim didn't follow him in. He felt like finding a hole to crawl into instead of his bed, which was probably short-sheeted and shaving-creamed anyway.

He'd hurt his best friend, who had only been trying to help him. What kind of kid was he, anyway?

A loser, that's what kind. Billy wasn't one, but he was. A kid who lets his whole camp down and then throws dirt in his best friend's face. Alone in the darkness, Tim lowered himself down onto the lowest front step and cried for a long time. Only when he heard the others coming back from supper did he run inside.

Billy was facedown on his bed in the darkness. Tim felt his own bed for damage, but it seemed to be okay. He lay down, still dressed, and within moments fell into an exhausted sleep.

The following night was the second social of the summer. Tim had been in a bad mood all day, going through the motions in softball, swimming, arts and crafts, and tennis on a rare day without basketball. If they'd had to play b-ball, he'd have felt even worse — every moment reminding him of his dismal failure of the day before.

The kids were speaking to him again, as if nothing had happened, but there was a certain coldness in their tone now, even the ones who had been fairly friendly to him before. Only Billy said not a word to him. Obviously waiting for an apology, Tim thought. Well, he'd apologized to him as soon as he'd said those horrible things. What did Billy want from him? Blood? Well, he wasn't going to get it. Tim felt bad enough about things already.

He'd forgotten about the social till lunch, when the

kids started talking about it in the mess hall. Then he thought about faking illness again, like he had at supper the night before. It might work, especially if he went to the infirmary and saw the nurse. Maybe he could steal one of those hot packs from her first-aid kit and fake having a fever. Anything not to have to deal with girls — not tonight. Not when he was feeling this bad about himself.

But Tito and Jody weren't taking no for an answer, and in the end, Tim went along, getting dressed up, moussing his hair, even shaving, although he didn't really need to yet. He walked to the gym at dusk like he was walking to a funeral. This, he was sure, was going to be total torture.

Tonight, the gym was decked out in an outer-space theme, with silver foil planets and stars hanging from the ceiling, twisting in the breeze from the fans, and shining colored lights reflected from disco balls rotating in various places around the hall.

The girls were all clumped around the food-and-drink table, just like last time. Some of the Condor boys were over there, trying to catch the girls' attention and impress them with how cool they were. Tim sat on one of the bleacher benches, trying to look casual.

"Yo, Daniels," Jody said, coming over and sitting down next to him. "Who do you like?"

"Me?"

"Is there another Daniels I don't know about?"

"What do you mean, who do I like?"

"You know — the girls, man. *Las chicas.*"

"Oh . . . I don't know . . . nobody special."

"You like that Wanda, right?" Jody said with a knowing smile. "I saw you two dancing last week."

"Yeah, Wanda's pretty cool," Tim said, just to get Jody off his back. Actually, he did kind of like Wanda, braces and all. At least she seemed really interested in him — not like Stephanie Krause, who kept giggling about him to her girlfriends and whispering about him to Mike Gruber.

He saw Stephanie now, her black hair gleaming red and blue in the soft lights of the gym. She was talking to not one, not two, but three guys, and when a new song started, she began dancing with one of them. It was a Condor boy — probably fifteen years old. Man, thought Tim. The oldest kids get to choose any girl they want to dance with.

He would have loved to ask Stephanie to dance. But after last time, he'd decided once and for all — no more asking girls to dance. If anyone wanted to dance with him, she could ask him. Maybe, maybe he'd say yes. But getting rejected was for the birds, and he felt bad enough already.

"Well, get on up there and find her, yo," Jody said, giving him an elbow.

"Sure, Jody," he said, getting up. Anything to get away from you and your nagging.

He waltzed over to the food-and-drink table, poured himself some punch, bopping in time to the music, and then edged slowly toward the side doors and through them, out onto the porch. Out here, there were a few couples whispering and kissing in the darkness.

Tim found an empty bench and sat down on it to sip his punch and wait out the evening — or as much of it as he could before anyone noticed he was missing.

He didn't know how long he'd been out there — maybe five or ten minutes — when he looked up and saw a dark shadow looming between him and the porch light. Even in the semidarkness, he could tell it was her — could tell by the shimmering of her black hair and the way she tossed it to the side as she approached him. "Hi, Tim," she said in that musical voice of hers. "It's me. Stephanie."

"Oh, hi," he said, his voice barely audible, so big was the lump in his throat. "What's up?"

"I saw you come out here, and I kind of wanted to talk with you. Could I, um, sit down?"

"Sure," Tim said, shoving over a little to make room for her on the small bench. Behind them, a big window would have given a view of the gym and the dancers, except that a white sunshade had been pulled down from inside. They were private out here. All the other couples were kissing. For goodness' sake, what was Stephanie doing out here? What did she want from him?

"You're not dancing tonight?" she asked softly.

"Um, nah, I kind of didn't feel like it."

"Bad day yesterday, huh?"

"You heard?"

"Kinda. Hey, it's okay, don't feel bad. The girls lost, too. We got creamed."

"You guys didn't have a ten-year winning streak to protect," Tim pointed out.

"Yeah, but so what?" Stephanie said. "Who cares about a dumb streak?"

She was being so nice! His head was spinning. What was going on here?

"I thought you were a good dancer," she said. "Last time, I mean. It was fun."

"Yeah?" He was finding it all hard to believe. Here she was, coming to him like an angel in his lowest moment, saying things to him he wouldn't have dared to dream of!

Still, the nagging doubts in his head wouldn't let him give in to the dream. "You — you were laughing at me last time," he said. "I saw you with your girl-friends."

"What? I was not!" she said, taken aback. "Why would I do that?"

He had no answer to that question. What was he going to say? Because I'm a loser?

"You were. You and Mike were whispering, and you were checking me out. I thought you — I thought he might have wanted you to ask me to dance, you know, as a goof."

"That is sick." Stephanie recoiled. "You are so totally wrong."

"Really?" She seemed so angry with him, and he didn't want her to be angry with him. Besides, why would she be angry if she was guilty?

"You want to know the truth? Mike's jealous of you," she whispered in his ear, giggling softly, making little hairs stand up on the back of his neck.

"How . . . how come? He's better than me at every sport there is."

"He thinks I like you, because I told him I thought you were cute. And it really ticked him off that I asked you to dance." She grinned mischievously, and her eyes twinkled at him.

"Oh . . ."

"Tim . . . have you ever kissed a girl?"

His heart took a long pause before starting to beat again, and he felt close to passing out.

"Um, sure," he lied. "I mean, once or twice."

"Oh," she said, sounding disappointed.

"Not really kissing, though," he said, hoping he hadn't blown his chance by saying the wrong thing. "Just kind of like, you know, pecks and stuff."

"Oh," she said, smiling and giggling again. "You wanna kiss?"

He swallowed hard and tried to say yes, but nothing came out, so he only nodded his head.

"Okay," she said, quickly looking over her shoulder

to make sure no one was watching. "Close your eyes, then."

She said it loudly, and he wondered why, but he was too wrapped up in what was about to happen to pay attention to anything else. He closed his eyes.

"Now kiss me," she whispered.

He moved his head slowly forward, lips first, reaching for hers. He felt them, soft and warm and . . . rubbery?

*Ffffffttttttt!* He opened his eyes in shock, only to see that he'd just kissed, not Stephanie Krause's lips, but a rubber whoopee cushion!

Laughter erupted from behind him. Turning, he saw that the sunshade had been lifted from inside, and six or seven kids were staring at him through the window, pointing and screaming with glee.

Tim could feel himself turning bright red. He wheeled around, but Stephanie was nowhere in sight.

Tim had had all he could stand. He marched straight off the porch and back to Eagles Nest, so angry that he was sure smoke must be coming out of his ears.

Billy arrived about fifteen minutes later. "What happened?" he asked. Apparently, he'd forgotten he was mad at Tim.

"They played a nasty trick on me," Tim said, not going into the gory details. "You were right about the kids here, Billy. They're the pits."

"So you finally got mad," Billy said, crossing his arms on his chest and nodding with satisfaction. "I was wondering how long it would take you to come around to my point of view."

"Well, I'm through getting mad," Tim said. "I say it's time we got even."

They lay in their beds in the dark that night, but neither Billy nor Tim dozed off. They remained awake and alert, listening to the low sounds of conversation coming from the other rooms of Eagles Nest, the boys talking and laughing softly about things that had happened at the social.

Tim knew — he just knew — that the laughter was at his expense. The whoopee-cushion stunt had caught him completely off guard. And Tim held one person, and one person alone, responsible — Mike Gruber.

He felt sure that Mike had put Stephanie up to it. It must have been him, because what reason did Stephanie have to hurt his feelings? Whereas Mike had had it in for Tim ever since Tim blew it in the game against Camp Chickasaw.

Maybe even before — Tim wondered if Stephanie

had asked him to dance that first time because she wanted to. He wanted to believe it was Stephanie's own idea — that she was telling the truth when she'd said he was cute — but he figured it was Mike all along, putting her up to it from the very start. He and the other kids had probably just gotten tired of taunting Billy and decided it was time to go after chicken boy's best friend.

"It's time," he heard Billy murmur. "Let's rock and roll."

Tim sat bolt upright and grabbed a plastic bucket from the floor. They'd borrowed it from the cleaning closet earlier so they wouldn't have to make a lot of noise now. Tim went to the bathroom and filled the bucket with warm water while Billy scouted the territory, watching for intruders, listening for the sounds of campers who were still awake. "The coast is clear," he whispered to Tim.

"Here I come," Tim whispered back. They made their way down the stairs, holding their breath with every creak of the old wooden steps. No one inside any of the little rooms stirred as they passed, even though some of them had their doors wide open.

They stopped in front of room five — the room shared by Brian Kelly and Mike Gruber. Tim and Billy nodded to each other, and Billy slowly turned the knob. The door opened with only a few minor creaks. Good thing they'd oiled it earlier, before the other kids came back from the social.

Tim put the bucket down at the side of Mike's bed. Then Billy gently took Mike's arm by the wrist and lowered his hand into the bucket of warm water. "Let's go!" he mouthed, not making any sound.

They left the room as quietly as they had come and didn't bother to shut the door behind them. Again, they held their breath till they nearly turned blue as they mounted the steps and tiptoed back to their room. Safe in their beds, they went to sleep smiling, knowing what was bound to come at the first light of day.

"AAARRRGH!"

"What happened?"

"What's going on?"

"Gruber wet the bed!"

"What? No way!"

"Yes way!"

"Shut up, you jerks, it's not funny!"

"Sorry, Mike."

"Sorry, Mike . . . you really did it, huh?"

"I said SHUT UP!"

Billy and Tim lay in bed, laughing to split a gut, then got up and high fived each other. But they wiped the smiles off their faces when they heard multiple foot-steps clunking up the stairs.

"You two are history!" Mike screamed as he barged through the door. "I'm gonna take you apart!"

"You're not gonna do anything," Jody said, grabbing Mike from behind and holding him in a bear hug. "You just calm down, Gruber."

"They stuck my hand in warm water!" he shouted, and Tim could see the tears of humiliation forming in Mike's eyes. "I'm gonna make them pay!"

"You're gonna do nothing, you hear? You dish it out, you gotta be able to take it." Jody spun Mike around and forced him to look him in the eye. "I want a promise from you right now, or you can go speak to Coach Gabe, okay?"

Gruber snarled, but relaxed his body. The immedi-ate threat, Tim could see, was over. Still, he knew Mike Gruber would remember who had given him his comeuppance. The battle was over — the war had just begun.

✿     ✿     ✿

The water trick was an old stunt Billy had read about in a book of practical jokes once. Tim was surprised the other kids hadn't already tried it on the two of them but thought it sounded like a great trick to play on his enemy — even if it was kind of cruel.

It turned out that with all the pranks that went on at Camp Wickasaukee, this one had never been tried on a camper over the age of ten before, let alone brought off successfully. Tim could understand why Mike was so upset — if it had been him, he would have been totally furious. It was even worse than kissing the whoopee cushion.

Mike continued to be sullen all that day, through basketball clinic, swimming, and soccer. Tim and Billy, on the other hand, were having their best day yet at camp. All of a sudden, the other kids were treating them with warmth and friendliness. Tim guessed that he and Billy had earned their respect, not just for striking back, but for pulling off such a big prank on such an untouchably popular kid.

Funny, though — the more slaps on the back they got about it, the more Tim felt guilty for sinking to their level. He was no longer angry — which was good, because last night, he'd been like a volcano ready to blow. But now that he was over it, Tim could see that he and Billy had started a feud that was going to last the rest of their four weeks here, and make it a totally miserable experience.

By the second afternoon, Tim had made up his mind to apologize to Mike Gruber and to try and turn the page on everything that had happened. He told Billy about it during letter-writing period, an hour before supper.

"Are you out of your gourd?" was Billy's response. "You seriously think he's gonna forgive you and want to be your best buddy from now on?"

"All I want," Tim responded, "is a truce."

"Yeah, well, good luck," Billy snorted. "Fat chance."

"I'm gonna go talk to him right now and apologize."

"What if he's not alone?"

"I don't care. If I have to say I'm sorry in front of everybody, I will."

"Suit yourself," Billy said. "But don't include me, because I'm not about to apologize. He deserved it if anybody ever did. Have you already forgotten what he did to you?"

"I'm not even sure he was responsible for that," Tim admitted. "It might have been her idea."

"Yeah, right," Billy sniffed. "And I had nothing to do with the other night."

"I won't say you did," Tim told him. "I'll take total responsibility."

"You're a nut," Billy said, shaking his head. "But thanks. Sorry I was mad at you before."

"Huh?"

"You know — when you laughed at me with the rest of them."

"Oh, yeah. Sorry for that. It was just . . . you know . . . kinda comical."

Billy smiled. "So was Gruber with that wet stain on his pajamas."

They both cracked up, but then Tim said, "I'm going now."

"Hey," Billy said. "Good luck."

"Thanks. I'm sure I'll need it."

He went downstairs and was about to knock on Mike's door, when there was a commotion outside on the front steps. "Get it! Get it!" kids were yelling, and the next thing Tim knew, a squirrel raced into the building. Its eyes were wide with panic as it zigzagged toward him, looking for a safe place to hide. In hot pursuit, in came seven or eight of the Eagles, some of

100

them carrying baseball bats and tennis racquets, yelling for squirrel blood.

Mike Gruber opened his door. "What the —?" he started to say, and then, everything happened in a blur. The squirrel raced up the stairs, and before anyone could react, there was a scream from Billy Futterman. "AAAAAHHH! Help! Help!" he cried. "There's a squirrel under my bed. Somebody help!"

Tim was up the stairs in a flash. He knew that squirrels could do incredible damage to walls, doors, windows, and furniture if they were on the loose and terrified. Unless they could confine it to a small space and then bag it with a net, it could totally trash Eagles Nest. He slipped into the room and slammed the door behind him.

There was a blood-curdling scream from the other side of the door. "Open the door!" kids were shouting. "Open it! Open it!"

"I can't!" Tim shouted back, leaning against the door with all his weight to keep the kids from forcing it open. "Go get a net. I've got it trapped in here!"

"You idiot," came Brian Kelly's voice. "You've got Gruber's finger trapped in the door!"

**11**

The finger was broken in two places. Mike Gruber came back from the infirmary with a cast on the finger and murder in his eyes. "You just wait till I'm out of this cast," he managed to say before he was restrained by Tito and led into his own room for a "calm-down" talking-to. "You'd better watch your back, Daniels!" were the last words Tim heard before the door slammed shut.

Dick Dunbar steered Tim back upstairs and into his room, a safe distance from the wounded but still dangerous Gruber. "He'll chill out after a while," Dick said, slapping Tim on the back. "I mean, you didn't do it on purpose, right?" He paused, which told Tim that he actually expected an answer.

"Of course not!" he said. "You actually think I —?"

"No, no, of course not," Dick said. "I just needed to hear it from you is all."

Tim sighed and slumped into his bedside chair. "I don't know why Mike hates me so much," he said.

"Well, you did break his finger."

"No, I mean before that. He's hated me practically since I got here."

"Why you?" Dunbar asked.

"I don't know," Tim said. "I guess because I was friends with Billy, and he didn't like Billy."

"When was the first time you remember him being hostile to you?"

"I guess since I blew the game against Chickasaw," Tim said. "Or maybe it was before that, at practice. I'm not sure. He might have been mad at me over this girl Stephanie."

"A girl, huh?" Dick said, his lips curling into a sly smile.

"Yeah, he's kind of going with her, but she asked me to dance," Tim said, letting Dick draw his own conclusions, and not bothering to tell him his own suspicions — that Stephanie had been egging Tim on from the start just for her and Mike's amusement.

"I see," said Dunbar. "Makes sense, kinda. Anyway, he's got even more to be mad about now."

"You mean his finger?"

"You bet. He's sidelined for the next two weeks at least. And because of that, guess who our new starting point guard is?"

Suddenly, it sank in. "Me?"

"You bet," Dunbar smiled, ruffling Tim's hair. "You da man. We've got another intercamp match day after tomorrow. Be ready."

"Who is it?"

"Camp Woodbine. Should be easy pickin's, but you never know. I think losing to Camp Chickasaw took a lot out of our guys. Killed the mystique, the aura, know what I mean?"

"Uh-huh."

"Hang in there, Tim," Dunbar advised as he got up to go. "Stay cool, and distribute the ball around. You'll be fine."

"Thanks," Tim said, but as the door closed behind Dick, he felt anything but fine. The weight of the world had just come crashing down on him. The whole camp would be watching him — the kid who took Mike Gruber out of contention — to see if he could measure up to Gruber's high standards.

If he failed . . .

Tim swallowed hard. He didn't even want to think about what would happen if he let the team down, and they lost another intercamp games because of him.

Tim had made up his mind. He'd had enough of getting revenge, on Mike Gruber or anybody else. It didn't make him feel any better, really, and it just made the other guy madder. Sooner or later, Tim would find himself the victim of Gruber's revenge, or whomever's, and the whole cycle would go on forever, or at least until Tim and Billy's last week here was up. No, revenge wasn't where it was at. Tim had decided that the way to show Gruber was to become the best point guard Camp Wickasaukee had ever had.

Of course, that was easier said than done. In his two-plus weeks here, Tim had already blown it big time by losing the game against Chickasaw. But from now on, as Dick Dunbar had said, he would be the Eagles starting point guard. He'd have a lot more minutes on the court to show what he could do. And

Tim was determined to make the most of his opportunity.

Camp Woodbine was supposed to be a pushover. At least, that's what the veteran campers all said. But something about the way they said it made Tim wonder. They sounded as if they were saying it to convince themselves of something they didn't really believe in their hearts.

Tim knew why, too. It was because the loss to Chickasaw had shaken their confidence. No longer was Camp Wickasaukee invulnerable. Superman had met kryptonite, and now, nothing was a sure thing — especially not with the great Mike Gruber sidelined. And that, of course, was Tim's fault, too.

He heard the nervousness in Jody's voice that morning as they prepared to take on Camp Woodbine. "This camp has never lost two intercamp games in one summer — never. And we've got the big rematch with Camp Chickasaw next week. So if you guys blow it today, and we get beat again next week . . . well, let's just say it better not happen, okay? Every kid who ever went to this camp is counting on you guys to come through today."

Well, thought Tim, that's easy for him to say. He

doesn't have to get out there and play. But he didn't say anything. All morning, as they battled Camp Woodbine in soccer (a 3–2 loss), swimming (a narrow victory), and softball (a lopsided win), Jody kept reminding them of what was at stake.

The basketball game was set to begin at 4 P.M., and by 3:30, the gym was already filling up with spectators. "We're up by two points," Tim heard Brian Kelly tell Mike Gruber as the two of them sat on the Eagles bench. Brian was suited up, but Mike was in jeans and a T-shirt. His eyes, shooting daggers of hatred, followed Tim wherever he went. It was almost more than Tim could stand.

He wanted to go over and speak to Mike, to tell him he was sorry, that he hadn't meant to break his finger. But he knew Mike wouldn't believe him — not after the warm-water stunt and all that business with Stephanie Krause.

They were only up by two points. The basketball game was worth five. This was it, and everybody knew it. Lose, and they'd set a record for failure that would probably live in infamy forever in Camp Wickasaukee lore. Win, and he could start to turn the page on all the bad stuff that had happened so far this summer.

Billy was now on the Eagles basketball team as an emergency replacement. Tim had lobbied for him with Jody the day before. "We need rebounding and shot blocking," he'd told him. "Tito says they have a kid who's six foot four."

"We've got Bobby Last," Jody had countered.

"Yeah, but what if he gets in foul trouble?"

"Hmmm. Maybe you're right. I'll think about it." And he had. He'd put Billy on the team, in spite of the howls of protest from the other kids.

The game began, and Tim stopped thinking about all the other things that were weighing on his mind. He concentrated on basketball alone, and so did the other Eagles. By halftime, they were up by 12 points and were looking good, except that Bobby Last had four fouls already.

"You're gonna have to sit for a while," Jody told Last.

"No, Coach," Bobby complained. "Put me in — I'll take it easy on him."

*Him* being the tall kid on the other team — the kid who had single-handedly kept his team in the game with 14 points, a ton of rebounds, and six blocked shots in the first half.

"Nope. Can't afford to lose you. Donnie — I'm

putting you on the big guy. Don't get in foul trouble, but stay on him as best you can." He turned to Tim. "You're doing good, Daniels. Keep it up. Just control the tempo. Remember, the clock is our friend. And take care of the ball. No turnovers."

"Right," Tim said, all business.

The whistle blew for the start of the second half, and Tim got up off the bench. As he headed back onto the court, he scanned the bleachers, looking to see if Mike Gruber was still there. He hadn't been on the bench at halftime, which was a surprise to Tim. He'd have thought Mike would still want to feel like a part of the team, even though he was injured.

And then he saw Mike and knew at once why he hadn't been on the bench. Gruber was in the last row of the bleachers, with his arm around Stephanie Krause's shoulder. When he saw Tim looking at them, he leaned over and kissed Stephanie right on the lips. And he kept it up for a long time, too. Tim stood there, ignoring the ref's whistle, until Brian Kelly came over and shook him. "Yo, shorty, are you in this game or not?"

"Huh? Oh, yeah," Tim said, feeling his face go red. "Yeah, I'm ready. Let's do it."

Woodbine won the tap, and went right to their big man. He worked his way in on Donnie D. and sank an easy layup. Donnie was a great player, but he was five inches shorter than this kid. There was no way he could stop him without fouling him. Tim knew he was going to have to ratchet up the offense, or Woodbine would come storming back on the shoulders of their giant center.

Tim took the inbounds pass and sped up the floor. He switched hands on the dribble, bounced it between his legs, and drove the lane, heading for the basket.

Now if that didn't impress Stephanie, nothing would.

*Bam!* The big kid in the middle swatted away his shot like it was a mosquito. The rebound resulted in a fast-break bucket the other way, and suddenly, the lead was down to 8.

Tim brought the ball upcourt again, determined this time to show Stephanie what he could do. He pictured himself back on the playground, dribbling circles around the other kids and sinking uncontested layups. But the Woodbine team was playing a zone here, and they were clogging the lane so much that Tim had to back it out to the high post.

He glanced over to the sidelines and saw Mike, still with his arm around Stephanie. Again, he leaned over and kissed her. And just then, Tim saw a blur going past him — it was the other team's point guard, robbing him of the ball and streaking downcourt for the uncontested layup Tim was supposed to have scored!

Now it was only a 6-point lead, and Jody yelled for time-out. "Daniels, take a seat," he told Tim, pointing to the bench. "Binkman, you're in."

Tim's face burned with shame as the third-string point guard, Steve Binkman, went into the game. Steve was a pretty good outside shooter, as Tim well knew from scrimmages and previous games, but he couldn't dribble to save his life! Why was Jody putting him in at point guard, the position that ran all the plays and handled the ball the most?

"Now look," Jody told Tim after play had resumed, "I want you to go back in there next whistle, but I want you to quit hogging the ball. You dish it, okay? Every time. I don't want you taking any shots, understand? No bricks from outside, no layups that get stuffed inside. You dish it to Donnie and make everyone clear out for him."

Tim nodded, grateful that Jody was giving him one more chance to redeem himself. When the whistle blew, there were only two minutes left in the game, and Wickasaukee had lost the lead. They were down by 3 points — not an impossible task — but so much was riding on an Eagles victory that it felt like they had to climb Mt. Everest.

Tim took the inbounds pass and called for a Brooklyn Three. Three meant Donnie, who was playing center for them now, with Last fouled out. Tim tossed it to Donnie, who tossed it right back, then spun off his man and headed toward the basket. Tim lofted the ball slowly over the surprised defender, and Donnie reached over his head to touch the pass and send it off the glass and into the basket.

It was a world-class play, and the entire bench and bleachers erupted in cheers. Those cheers rose even higher when Donnie stole the ball and drove to the hoop again, finishing it with a slam dunk!

They had the lead now, but not for long. Woodbine's center had the ball and was backing Donnie up toward the basket. The giant turned and laid a soft hook right through the hoop.

Tim took a quick glance at the clock and saw that he had only thirty seconds to work with. He knew he needed to waste a lot of it, so that the Eagles' next shot would be the game's last. Tim didn't want to give Camp Woodbine a chance to come back down the floor.

He dribbled until they came out after him, then dished off to Donnie. Now it was DeGeronimo's turn to do his magic. He spun one way, then the other, faked the shot, and the giant, who had leapt into the air, crashed down on Donnie's shoulders. The ref's whistle blew, and Donnie went to the line for two foul shots.

With the crowd screaming, cheering him on, he sank the first. But the second shot caromed off the rim and to the right. Tim went after it like a cat and grabbed the rebound away from two Woodbine players. He sprung into the air and led Donnie, who was cutting for the basket. Donnie grabbed the ball in midstride and laid it up and in, just as the final buzzer sounded. They'd won the game, by 2 points. And Tim had contributed the winning assist!

Everyone on the Eagles leapt into each others' arms and danced up and down on the court, as the defeated Woodbine team shuffled off in defeat. Tim tried to spot Gruber and Stephanie in the crowd. Had she seen him in his finest moment? Or had she been too busy kissing Mike?

He couldn't find them, and now his teammates were slapping him on the back, congratulating him for a job well done. He was glad for the recognition — after all, he'd been after it for weeks — but the sight of Mike and Stephanie kissing had left him with an empty feeling in the pit of his stomach. And the fact that he'd pretty much blown the game before coming back in to help save it took something away from the moment. It was a victory all right, but a bittersweet one. He'd have to do much better next week, when Camp Chickasaw blew back in for the big rematch.

**12**

**S**o you think you're all that now, huh?"

Tim stared into the angry green eyes of Mike Gruber and didn't know how to answer him.

"You think you won the big game, so now you're the cheese?" Gruber pushed open the door of Tim's room, and Tim backed away to let him enter. "That was a team we should have beaten by forty points, yo. And if you hadn't broken my finger, we would have."

"It was an accident, Mike, I swear it," Tim assured him, but Mike just kept coming, and Tim kept retreating till, with a shove of his hand, Mike pushed Tim down on the bed and stood glowering down at him.

"Sure," he said. "No sweat, man. You didn't mean it. You just kept pushing on that door even after we told you to stop, because you wanted to save that poor little squirrel, right?"

"I didn't say that . . . ," Tim began, but Mike didn't want to hear his explanations.

"And making me wet my bed," Mike said. "That was an accident, too?"

"Well . . . actually, I feel really bad about that one," Tim said. "It's just — well, you know, after the thing you and Stephanie pulled on me —"

"Stephanie's mine, understand?" Mike interrupted. "Just stay away from her."

"What?" What was Mike talking about? Of course Stephanie was his girlfriend. It wasn't like she liked Tim or anything . . . was it?

No, come on. What was he thinking? "I'll stay away from her," he assured Mike. "Why would I want to talk to her anyway, after what she did to me?"

"You deserved it," Mike growled. "You deserve a lot worse. Watch out or you'll get it, too."

He turned on his heel and walked out of the little room, leaving Tim staring after him.

It was one thing to beat a team like Woodbine, with only one really dangerous player. It was another thing to beat Chickasaw, a team that played ferocious de-

116

fense and could score at will if you didn't stick to them like glue.

If they lost to Chickasaw again, Tim would be right back in the doghouse. And he knew if he didn't pick up his game between now and then, that was exactly what would happen.

So he was totally psyched when Tito came back to Eagles Nest and announced that the NBA players would be arriving the next day for the annual summer clinic. Especially when he heard that one of the players coming was Allister Edwards. Tim had watched Edwards play for years, leading his team to the NBA finals twice. Watching the games on TV wasn't nearly as much fun since Edwards had retired two seasons ago.

If anybody could help him become the best point guard Wickasaukee had ever seen, it had to be Allister Edwards! But in a one-day clinic, how could he make sure he got enough of Edwards's time and attention?

The morning featured the NBA stars doing their warm-ups — sinking shot after shot from beyond the arc and behind the foul line, performing incredible spin dunks and behind-the-back passes as they went through their everyday routines.

Then Charlie Jansen, the legendary onetime coach of the Sixers, had the players demonstrate key fundamentals. He called up several volunteers from the audience — but he never called on Tim, whose arm threatened to pull free from its socket, he raised it so high and so often.

The morning session ended with the campers doing their drills and the NBA stars and coaches watching and giving guidance. "Roll it off your fingertips!" one of them told Tim after he bricked a jump shot off the backboard. "And give it a higher arc." Tim had to go around to the back of the line after his shot, though, and he didn't get the chance to take several in a row and get it right.

He was beginning to despair of getting any time at all with Allister Edwards. Then, at lunch, Tito told him and Gruber to shove over to each side, to make room for a guest. Tim nearly swallowed his tongue when he saw that it was none other than the man he wanted to talk to most in the whole wide world.

For most of lunch, Mike Gruber didn't shut up, talking up a storm and hogging all Edwards's attention. But Mike seemed more interested in talking about how great he was himself than he did in learning anything.

Finally, Dick Dunbar spoke up. "You know, Al," he said, "Mike's a super point guard, and him getting injured hurts us a lot. We've got Tim here filling in, but he could use a few tips on how to approach the big game we've got coming up. Any words of wisdom?"

Tim could have hugged Dick, he was so grateful. And now, Allister Edwards turned and saw him as if for the first time. "Well," he asked Tim, "what've you got?"

"I beg your pardon?"

"What are your skills, your good tools — what've you got workin'?"

Tim didn't know what to say. He didn't want it to sound like he was bragging, the way Mike had been doing for the past half hour. But the way Edwards had asked the question, how could he help it?

Again, Dick Dunbar rode to the rescue. "Good on the dribble," he said, "got the moves, drives the lane well."

"Mmm-hmm," said Edwards, stroking his chin. "Tell you what, Tim — after we finish eating, let's you and I go out and shoot a few hoops. What do you say?"

"I say yes!" Tim said, grinning from ear to ear.

"You've got to think like you're a magnet, see?" Edwards told him, dribbling the ball as he talked. "You're

119

always thinking, 'How can I get those guys to come at me?' Then, when they do, you dish it off to the man they just left. You're always looking to dish off, not to score. You only shoot when they leave you alone and bunch up the middle."

Tim drank it all in, trying not so much to memorize everything Edwards said, which would have been impossible, as to understand the way he thought out there on the court.

"Sometimes you've got to drive the lane to draw attention," Edwards went on. "Then you're looking behind you for the free man."

"Looking behind me?" Tim repeated, confused.

"You've got to open the eyes in the back of your head, man!" Edwards said with a laugh. "Look where they are before you drive."

"Oh, I get it! Sure, makes sense."

"Remember," Edwards said as they wound up their session, "a point guard's job is not to do all the scoring — it's to make your teammates better. Oh, and one more thing."

"Yes?"

"You'd better work on that jump shot of yours. Unless you make that a serious threat, nobody's gonna come out to play you up high."

"But I've never been a good outside shooter, really." Tim looked down, feeling suddenly doubtful.

"You get Dunbar to work with you. He's got himself a pretty shot. Get him to spend the whole day with you on it tomorrow, and you'll be ready for that big game."

Dick Dunbar was standing at the foul line waiting for Tim in the gym the next morning after breakfast. "I understand I'm on special duty today," he said with a grin, chest-passing the ball to Tim.

"I really appreciate this," Tim told him, launching a shot.

"Well, there, see," Dick said, retrieving the ball, "you didn't set your feet before you shot. Now let's start with ten shots, and set your feet each time. Then square your body to the basket —"

"But it takes so long!" Tim protested. "What if I can't get the time or the space to do that?"

"Well then, you don't take the shot," Dick said flatly. "Simple as that."

They worked for an hour straight, without taking a

break. Dunbar showed him how to balance the ball in his hand as he rose to his jump, how to roll it gently off the fingertips with a high arc, how to make sure his jump was straight into the air, and when in the jump to release the ball.

By the end of the day, Tim had set a new personal record of twelve straight foul shots made. He'd sunk three straight 3-pointers twice and could feel the rhythm of the shot in a way he never had before.

"Boy, when I signed up to come here," he told Dick as they left the gym, "I never thought I'd get a whole day of private lessons."

"Lucky break," Dick Dunbar said, then grinned at his own dry humor. "Break, get it? Oooo, shouldn't have said that, I guess. Poor Mike. Well, hey, I don't believe you meant to break his finger."

"You don't?"

"Course not. You didn't even know who was on the other side of that door."

"I told Mike that, but he didn't believe me," Tim said.

"Well, you can understand how he might be feeling."

"Sure."

"Don't feel too bad for Mike. He's been coming here seven years now, and I'll bet you that five of those years, he was the one getting the private coaching. It's time somebody else got the chance. And it might as well be you as anybody, right?"

The night before the big rematch with Camp Chickasaw, all of Wickasaukee, boys and girls, held a huge pep rally around the campfire. They roared cheers into the night that echoed off the hills and back to them again. They promised to try their best, never to quit until the game was over, and to do honor to the great tradition of Camp Wickasaukee. That meant, of course, restoring the winning tradition by proving that their only loss had been a fluke. This was going to be the big match of the summer, and everyone knew it.

Tim sat quietly through most of the cheers, deep into his own thoughts. Then he stared across the campfire at Billy, who at least was joining in, shouting with all the rest of them.

Billy. His oldest and best friend. He hadn't been so great to Billy the past three weeks. And why not?

Because he'd been too busy trying to impress these other kids, who didn't even care about him, kids he'd never see again after the game was over. To try to win Mike Gruber's friendship, he'd turned against the one kid here who would still be his friend when camp was over.

He wanted to do something to repay Billy for sticking with him in spite of the way he'd acted. Something big, to make a statement not just to Billy, but to all the other kids as well. He went over and sat beside his friend, patting him on the knee. "Hey, Bill," he said. "How're you doing?"

Billy shrugged. "I hate this cheering stuff," he said. "It makes my ears ring for days after."

"Listen," Tim said, staring into the fire. "You listening?"

"Sure," Billy said, leaning forward. "What?"

"I'm going to get you the ball tomorrow."

"Huh?"

"You're going to score the winning bucket."

"What are you talking about?"

"I'm telling you right now, Billy — just be ready. I'll give you the nod, and then the ball will be coming at

124

you. Don't think twice — just lay it up and into the hoop."

"Tim, wait a minute —"

But Tim was already up and walking. It didn't matter anyway — nothing Billy could have said, then or later, would have changed his mind. Billy was going to score the winning bucket in the biggest game of the summer. Tim was going to see to it.

**13**

**T**he tension was so thick in the mess hall the next morning that Tim could barely breathe. Nobody was doing much talking. Each camper was in his own thoughts, trying to focus on what he could do to win the match for Wickasaukee. Worst of all was the sense of fear filling the hall — fear of what would happen if they didn't do their best, if they messed up at the crucial moment.

Nobody should have felt this more than Tim, of course. He was the one who'd made that last, crucial mistake against Chickasaw two weeks ago. But somehow, he wasn't affected by it. He felt calm and quiet inside. He was going to do what Allister Edwards and Dick Dunbar had coached him to do — hit his shots from outside early, then look to dish to the open man.

Except that Tim, instead of looking for Donnie DeGeronimo or Bobby Last, was going to look for, and find, Billy Futterman — the last kid Chickasaw would be watching for.

"Please," Billy begged him when Tim reminded him of his intention as they finished their eggs. "This is a really bad idea. I'll only blow the shot, Tim."

"I don't care," Tim told him. "You're my best friend, and I say you're going to get the ball and win it for us."

"You're nuts," Billy said. "Everyone's gonna hate me when I blow it."

"If you blow it, wait a couple days and we'll be going home, and you'll never have to see these kids again. But guess what? You won't blow it. You'll see."

"I've already seen. In my nightmares."

"Breathe, Billy. Breathe. It's gonna be okay. Trust me."

Tim didn't know why, but he felt as sure of his words as he'd ever felt about anything in his life.

The morning went badly for Wickasaukee. In baseball and in soccer, Chickasaw came from behind to erase big home-team leads. Tim won his 200-yard dash, and Billy won two events in swimming, so they were personally coming up big early, keeping their camp in the hunt. Tim's back was sore by lunch, after getting slapped by so many of his bunkmates. Only Mike Gruber stayed clear of him.

By the time of the big basketball game, word went around that Wickasaukee was down by 4 points. The game was worth 5 in the standings. It all came down to this. To me, Tim thought. The starting point guard — the kid with the ball, and the game, in his hands.

He warmed up, hitting shot after shot from all different angles, not letting the tension or the noise get to him. Good, he thought. Now if only I can hit them with men guarding me . . .

The game began, and Billy, of course, was sitting way at the end of the bench. Tim took the ball off the opening tip from Bobby Last, and the Eagles were off to the races. Tim dribbled to the high post, pulled up, and launched a jumper perfectly off his fingertips — swish!

Back came Chickasaw with 2 points of their own on a layup that Bobby Last couldn't stop, earning a foul in the process. It was the start of a bad game for Bobby, who by halftime was riding the bench with four fouls.

Donnie DeGeronimo, on the other hand, was taking it to the hoop every time Tim got him the ball.

When he couldn't, Tim would pass off, find a free spot, call for the pass, and shoot it. He could feel his rhythm and was squaring his shoulders and jumping straight up, just like Edwards and Dick Dunbar had told him.

Their advice had been good. Tim hit five of his first six shots, two of them from 3-point range. With three of four foul shots added, he'd scored 15 points by the half! Donnie had 13, the next highest scorer. Tim took high-fives all along the bench, and when he got to Billy, he pointed a finger at him, as if to say, "Remember what we talked about."

Billy rolled his eyes, and who could blame him? He hadn't played the entire first half, even with Last riding the bench. When was Jody ever going to put him into the game? And if he didn't, how was Tim going to find him with the ball?

Wickasaukee had a 5-point lead going into the second half. But Jody's whole team was in foul trouble, not just Bobby Last. Donnie had three, and so did Brian Kelly. With those three guys out, Jody would be reduced to just one more big man off the bench — Billy Futterman. Still, he threw his starters back out there for the second half, yelling, "No fouls!" as if they needed reminding.

Tim had played the whole first half, and he was back in now. But he switched his entire approach for the second half. Instead of looking to shoot, he would now fake the shot, draw the defenders to him, and find his teammates for the open shot.

The strategy worked beautifully, as time after time, Tim found the others for easy points. Now it was the Chickasaw players who were getting in foul trouble.

But then, with six minutes left and Wickasaukee leading by 10, Bobby Last fouled out. Brian Kelly went in for him and notched his fifth foul just two minutes later. "Futterman, get in there," Jody barked. Billy, elbowed into action by the kid sitting next to him, got up and trotted onto the court.

Now Chickasaw mounted their biggest run of the game. With a minute left, they had crawled back to within 1 point. Then, on a drive, their center drew Donnie DeGeronimo into his fifth foul! Donnie threw a towel violently to the floor as he sat down. Tim thought he saw tears in Donnie's eyes as the Chickasaw center sank both his free throws to put his camp into the lead for the first time in the game.

Forty-two seconds left. 57–56 Chickasaw. Tim with the ball. He dribbled downcourt, slowing down to pull time off the clock. "Go to the hoop!" he heard Jody yell. He knew Jody wanted them to score right away, so they could get another shot at scoring if Chickasaw made a bucket. But Tim had other ideas — and he had the ball, so what he said went.

With ten seconds left on the clock, and the Chickasaw bench doing the countdown to victory, Tim drove the lane, executing a sharp spin move to split the defense. He leapt up as if to shoot, saw the Chickasaw center's arm come up to block the shot — and passed it between the opposing player's legs, bouncing it off the floor to Billy Futterman, who was standing behind the clump of players surrounding the basket.

Billy was all alone with the ball while the crowd chanted, "Three, two —"

"SHOOT!" Tim yelled — screamed, really. And it seemed to jar Billy out of his confusion, because he threw the ball up off the backboard — and into the hoop! *Swish!* Nothin' but net!

The whistle blew. Game over. Wickasaukee 58, Chickasaw 57!

"I told you! Didn't I tell you?" Tim shouted in Billy's ear as they danced around in a circle under the basket.

"I did it. I can't believe I did it!" Billy kept saying

over and over. And then they were mobbed by their teammates, and the whole mountain of humanity tumbled onto the gym floor.

The noise was deafening. It washed over Tim like a welcome rain after a long drought. He'd done it. He'd accomplished what he came here for.

He was ready to go home now.

He and Billy left for home two days later. Their four weeks at Wickasaukee had come to an end, and they were leaving now with mixed feelings.

Their last days at camp had been like a dream come true. Everyone was their friend. Billy's reputation was redeemed, and when kids laughed, they laughed with him, not at him.

As for Tim, he was the hero of the week. Coach Gabe made him rise from his chair at supper in the mess hall and get a standing ovation, with kids banging their forks and knives on the tables. Tim knew he was blushing, but he didn't care. It was an awesome feeling to be the hero. I could get used to this, he told himself.

But he knew he'd better not. He knew there'd be losing as well as winning in his future, and he was ready for that. If Billy had missed the big shot, it would have been a different ending here at camp for the two of them, but it would have been all right with Tim. As far as he was concerned, he'd done the right thing as he saw it. That was what really mattered in the end. And that was how he was determined to play it from now on.

On pickup day, he was waiting in the parking lot, sitting on his duffel bag and looking to see if one of the arriving cars was his parents' minivan. Billy was off at the canteen, stuffing his pockets with snacks for the long drive home, spending his last dime on junk food. So Tim was by himself when he spotted a lone figure walking toward him out of the morning sun. As the figure came closer, he recognized her and swallowed hard.

"Hi, Tim," said Stephanie.

"Hi."

"You're leaving, huh?"

"Yup."

"I heard. That's why I came over. I wanted to say good-bye."

"Oh yeah? Why?"

"Don't be like that," she said, sitting down next to

133

him on his duffel bag. "I only played that trick on you because Mike made me do it."

"He *made* you?" Tim said skeptically. "How could he do that?"

"You know, he kept bugging me and bugging me till I said okay. I think he was ticked at you for losing that basketball game."

"And . . . ?"

"And you know, I was going with him, kind of, at the time, so . . ."

"So you agreed to do it, but you didn't really want to."

"Exactly!" She smiled at him, and for a second, he felt himself softening toward her.

"But now that you're leaving, I wanted to tell you how sorry I was."

"Okay. Apology accepted."

"And, oh — here's my number," she said, pressing a piece of paper into his hand. "You only live, like, half an hour from me, right?"

"Yeah, about that."

"So if you want to call me sometime, you know, like after the summer . . . I mean, we could go out or something."

"Okay," Tim said. "Maybe I will."

"Okay. Great!"

She gave him a quick peck on the cheek and sprang up to go. After a few steps, she stopped and looked at him over her shoulder. "Talk to you then, huh?"

"Right."

"Bye."

"Bye."

She walked off into the morning sun. He slowly crumpled the piece of paper, throwing it into a nearby trash can. He had no intention of ever calling Stephanie Krause, as attracted as he was to her. He forgave her for hurting his feelings. But if he was going to date a girl, he wanted it to be someone he could really trust.

"Hey," Billy said, coming back with his pockets bulging and bags of snacks in both hands. "Who was that?"

"That? Oh, that was Stephanie."

"Oh . . . uh-huh . . . and?"

"And what?"

Billy blinked. "Uh . . . nothing. Hey, there's your mom and dad!"

✿     ✿     ✿

All the long ride home, Tim basked in the memory of the past four weeks. It hadn't all been fun, not by a long shot. But he'd learned a lot, and he'd grown a lot. His game was better for sure. But above all, he knew now how important it was to have true friends and to be true to himself.

"Hey, Billy," he said, reaching over. "Let us have some of those chips."

# Matt Christopher®

Lance Armstrong

Kobe Bryant

Terrell Davis

Julie Foudy

Jeff Gordon

Wayne Gretzky

Ken Griffey Jr.

Mia Hamm

Tony Hawk

Grant Hill

Ichiro

Derek Jeter

Randy Johnson

Michael Jordan

Mario Lemieux

Tara Lipinski

Mark McGwire

Greg Maddux

Hakeem Olajuwon

Shaquille O'Neal

Alex Rodriguez

Briana Scurry

Sammy Sosa

Venus and
Serena Williams

Tiger Woods

Steve Young

## Read them all!

*Originally published as *Crackerjack Halfback*

Look Who's Playing First Base

Miracle at the Plate

Mountain Bike Mania

No Arm in Left Field

Nothin' but Net

Olympic Dream

Penalty Shot

Pressure Play

Prime-Time Pitcher

Red-Hot Hightops

The Reluctant Pitcher

Return of the Home Run Kid

Roller Hockey Radicals

Run, Billy, Run

Run for It

Shoot for the Hoop

Shortstop from Tokyo

Skateboard Renegade

Skateboard Tough

Snowboard Maverick

Snowboard Showdown

Soccer Duel

Soccer Halfback

Soccer Scoop

Spike It!

The Submarine Pitch

Supercharged Infield

The Team That Couldn't Lose

Tennis Ace

Tight End

Too Hot to Handle

Top Wing

Touchdown for Tommy

Tough to Tackle

Wheel Wizards

Windmill Windup

Wingman on Ice

The Year Mom Won the Pennant

All available in paperback from Little, Brown and Company